MW01240814

1

I'll

Never

Tell...

by

Anna Vucica

Dedicated to:

Howard Filiere who will truly be missed

and

The Cleveland Police

Thanks to the "Salon," Charlain, Peyton, and the rest of my friends who continue to support me!

Special Thanks

to my parents

Veselko and Mila Sabljic

Preface

Five years ago, Anthony's life was ruined. He was arrested for the murders of three young women. All women that he knew, but, did not kill. For five years, he sat in his jail cell thinking of nothing but of how he was arrested and how someone had set him up to take the fall. But why? Why him? He had one goal in mind and that was to find out the answers to these two questions. As far as he knew, he didn't have any enemies, and because of the conviction, he only had two friends left.

Chapter 1

It was June 29th, and another hot and humid day in Cleveland. Anthony was dripping from sweat as he walked to his parked car from the building where he worked. Two police officers lingered by his car. As he approached one of the officers asked,

"Anthony Rozman?"

"Yes," Anthony replied as the other officer walked behind him and pushed him against the car. His face burned from the hot car as his head was slammed against the hood. The officer grabbed his wrists and cuffed them behind his back. "What are you doing? What's going on?" he yelled as the officer who cuffed him read him his rights. "Murder?!" he said, shocked at what he was hearing. "I didn't murder anyone! You have the wrong guy! I am telling you I didn't do it!" He kept yelling as the officers pushed him in the back of the squad car and slammed the door.

Anthony Rozman was arrested for killing three young women in Cleveland, Ohio. The trial took about three weeks and Anthony didn't stand a chance. The prosecutor presented to the jury all of the evidence, which included a knife that was used in the three stabbings, and a key witness who helped to convict him. He was appointed a lawyer because he couldn't afford one and everything that could have possibly gone wrong, had. He was sentenced to life in prison without parole.

After serving four years at a maximum security prison, a man by the name of Norman Howser, moved by guilt, had found it within himself to help set Anthony free. Norman Howser, who was the only witness to testify at the trial, had confessed to lying on the stand, and had admitted that he was paid to say that he saw Anthony Rozman kill one of the women. His testimony was ruled out, and a year later, Anthony was released from prison.

He walked out on to the sidewalk, and breathed in the cold air of freedom as he looked back at the prison one last time. *Finally,*

I'm out of the hellhole, he thought to himself as he began to walk towards a parked silver BMW sedan. It was mid-March, and there was still too much snow covering the cold sidewalk. He took his time walking as the snow melted under his white sneakers and turned it into slush. He felt a drop trickle down his neck and then another. It started snowing again.

It was cold outside, so she didn't step out of the car to greet him. She watched him stroll down the sidewalk, and as he came closer to the car, Lisa unlocked the door and Anthony got in.

"Hi, Lisa," he said to her as he leaned in to give her a kiss on the cheek.

"Hi, yourself," she replied as she smiled at him. "How are you feeling? Are you excited?"

"I feel great. I have waited for this day for so long," he sighed. "I can't wait to get back to my life."

"Your wish is my command." She turned on the car and started the two hour drive.

Five years ago, Anthony's life was ruined. He was arrested for the murders of three young women. All women that he knew, but, did not kill. For five years, he sat in his jail cell thinking of nothing but of how he was arrested and how someone had set him up to take the fall. But why? Why him? He had one goal in mind and that was to find out the answers to these two questions. As far as he knew, he didn't have any enemies, and because of the conviction, he only had two friends left.

--------*-------*-------

Robert Tucker sat in his office at the third district police station on Chester Avenue. He couldn't believe that the man he put behind bars was let loose today. *That damn lawyer, Lisa Furrow.* He didn't think that she would be able to do it. Norman had sent her a letter of confession that she presented to a judge who set Anthony free. When the officers went to Norman's house to arrest him and charge him for lying under oath, they found him sitting in a chair, with blood oozing down his face and on to his plaid shirt. He had shot himself in the head. With the gun in hand, and a note on the table next to the wooden rocking chair, they ruled it as a suicide.

Robert Tucker knew who the real killer was and that was one secret that he planned on taking to the grave. He didn't get all that he wanted to achieve by sending Anthony Rozman to prison, but the promotion to lieutenant did compensate for some of it.

--------*--------*-------

Lisa looked over at Anthony who was slouched on the passenger seat. His eyes were closed, and without wanting to disturb him, she looked back ahead on the now white, slippery road. It was usually a two and a half hour drive from Columbus to Cleveland, but with the heavy snowfall coming down, they would be lucky if they made it in three. She had an apartment downtown with an extra bedroom that Anthony will be able to use. At least until he finds his own place. She is an only child and has never shared anything with anyone before. It will be pretty hard for her to give up her space, but hopefully it wouldn't be for too long. Her favorite song was on the radio. She turned it up and started to sing

"... it's all about the bass, 'bout that bass, no treble, it's all about the bass..."

Anthony opened his eyes and started to laugh.

"I take it you like this song?"

"It happens to be my favorite," she replied without looking at him and turned the radio up even louder. She sang the whole song and when it was over she turned the radio back down again. "What did you think of the song?"

"Not my style of music. I'm more into rock and roll," he replied. "How much longer 'til we get to your place? I can't wait to take a shower, eat something, and then actually sleep in a real bed again." Lisa glanced at the time on the dashboard. It was 1:45 p.m.

"We'll be there in twenty more minutes," she replied and smiled. The snow had disappeared since she got on I-71. Cleveland's unpredictable weather had never failed to amaze her.

"You know, I truly appreciate what you did for me, and what you are doing for me now. I can never thank you enough. I am forever indebted to you, Miss Furrow," Anthony said as he watched her stare ahead on the road.

"Not a problem Anthony. I am happy to help you." She smiled at him. *It is the least I could do for the mistake I have made.* Over the years, Lisa and Anthony had become close friends. She had visited him often while he was in prison and she had made it her mission to somehow get him out of there. She knew that he didn't commit the murders and trusted him enough to let him stay with her.

Lisa drove off the Innerbelt on 9th Street and headed north to her apartment. She was lucky that she had wealthy parents and could afford living in such a luxurious place. Her apartment was on the nineteenth floor and the views were spectacular. The apartment has an open floor plan with a spacious kitchen. There are two bedrooms and two bathrooms, so she was still able to have a sense of freedom.

Her father is a real estate developer who made millions before the real estate business declined. He bought a lot of property, mainly in the North Ridgeville and Avon Lake area, and has made many residential developments. Her mother has been a stay-at-home mom whom Lisa thinks more of as a child. After she was born, her mom had two miscarriages and just wasn't blessed with another child. Her mom has turned to drinking and has been taking antidepressant medicine for the last 10 years. Luckily, Lisa had her father, who always looked out for her.

Lisa graduated from Cleveland State University, John Marshall School of Law, and is now a divorce attorney with her own practice. While she was attending law school she was interested in becoming a criminal law attorney. Little did she know that the trial that she was observing was going to change her outlook on life. She sat in the courtroom, every day for three weeks, watching Anthony Rozman's life fall apart. After the verdict, she was disappointed, so much so, that she devoted all of her free time to helping Anthony get out of prison. She then realized that she could never be able to defend a criminal, nor would she be able to help put an innocent man behind bars. Criminal law, she decided then, was not for her.

She is 5ft. 3 in. tall, and has brown hair with blond highlights that, when not tied up, lies to just above her slender shoulders. She has light brown eyes that sometimes turn almost hazel depending on her mood.

Lisa unlocked the door to her apartment and motioned for Anthony to come in.

"Wow," he said as he walked into the spacious room. "This is amazing!" He walked over to the large windows and looked out over the city. Cleveland is as beautiful as he remembered it. Lisa showed him around and once he had seen it all, they sat down on the black leather couches in the living room.

"I took the day off tomorrow, thinking that I'll drive you around. I do have an extra car at my dad's place, which we can pick up tomorrow. I also think that we need to do some shopping as well. The only clothes you have are the ones you are wearing. Since its only 2:30, we can hit the mall and grab dinner on our way back."

"That sounds like a good plan." He felt horrible that he didn't have a penny to his name. The government will give him a settlement, but he wasn't sure when that check would come. "Lisa, I really appreciate this, as soon as I get the money I will pay you back. I've talked with Howard, and the company will hire me back. I will start working on Monday. I really don't plan on staying here too long."

"Don't worry about that stuff yet, I know you will pay me back. So let's hit the road and do some shopping!"

Bundled up in their coats, they walked to her car and headed toward the Great Northern Mall. They hit almost every department store, and Lisa took great pleasure in helping Anthony pick out a whole new wardrobe. He is tall, 6ft 2in, has a lean body, and has short, brown hair that is almost like a crew cut. His bangs are just long enough for him to spike them up with gel. He has light brown eyes and an amazing smile. He always disliked shopping and was glad that Lisa was with him. After two hours of walking around and carrying all those bags, they stopped at the food court to grab dinner. They both got the chicken teriyaki from the Asian vendor and took a seat at one of the empty tables. It was Thursday evening, and the mall was practically empty.

"This is one of the best meals I've had in quite a while," Anthony smiled and practically devoured the whole plate of food.

"I like the chicken teriyaki, too," she said. "We still need to hit one more place."

"Huh?!" he said in a whiny voice. "I think I have everything I need."

"We still need to get you a couple of suits, dress shirts, ties, and shoes. You are starting work on Monday and you need to look really good." He frowned. "Don't worry. It won't take us much longer." She grabbed his empty paper plate and hers, which was still half full, and threw it in the trash can. "Come on." She grabbed his hand and pulled him up to his feet like a little kid being forced to do something that he didn't want to do. They finally finished the shopping and headed back home. It was eight in the evening, but it was so dark it seemed as if it was much later.

He put all of his belongings in the closet and when he was done, he went to the living room and sat next to her on the couch. She was cuddled up in a blanket and was reading a book.

"You read a lot?" he asked her.

"As much as I can. It happens to be my favorite pasttime," she answered without taking her eyes off the book.

"I guess I'll let you read and go to bed then. Good night, Lisa, and thanks again."

"Good night," she replied and looked up to see him entering his bedroom. She watched him close the door and she exhaled. She was pretty nervous about Anthony staying here.

Chapter 2

He woke up to a pleasant aroma he hasn't smelled in a long time. *Is that what I think it is? Is it bacon? Eggs?* He quickly got out of bed and put on a sweatshirt and jeans. He then proceeded straight to the bathroom. A few minutes later, he was in the kitchen watching Lisa put the eggs and bacon on a plate.

"It smells so good in here," he smiled and sat at the table that was right by the window. It was a tall glass table that had two high chairs. "Is this okay?" he asked her, not sure if that was where he was supposed to sit. There was one more, huge wooden table that seats 12 situated a little farther down from this one.

"That's fine," she answered as she came to the table with two plates and a basket of toast. She put one in front of him and one on the other side. "I'll be right back." She walked back to the kitchen and grabbed the grape jelly and cream cheese out of the large stainless steel fridge. She sat down and started to spread the grape jelly (her favorite) on a piece of toast.

"This is great. So you know how to cook, too?! Is there anything you don't know how to do?" he asked and she blushed.

"I would consider myself a jack of all trades and a master of none type of person."

"I would say you are perfect," Lisa blushed again and responded, "a perfect person doesn't exist. I, however, do the best that I can to achieve perfection."

"So then you are a perfectionist?"

"Yes," she paused, "yes I am." Her phone rang and she looked at it to see who was calling. "Excuse me." She moved away from the table and answered the phone.

"Hi, hot stuff." She was happy that Jo had called her.

"How are you?" Her best friend, Jo, asked her. "Everything go okay last night?"

"Yes, it did," Lisa replied. "I will take him to my dad's to pick up the extra car after breakfast. Do you want to meet up for lunch or dinner?"

"Yes, let's do dinner. I will bring Bob and you bring Anthony. I am dying to meet him!" Jo exclaimed. "How about we meet at Marie's at about 7 tonight?"

"Perfect, will see you then." Lisa hung up the phone and returned to the table.

"Sorry, had to answer." Lisa said to Anthony, who was already finished eating. "Would you like some more?" she asked as she continued to eat.

"No thanks, I am stuffed."

Once she finished eating, she asked him if he was ready to go to her dad's to pick up her other car.

"Where does your dad live?"

"He lives in Rocky River. We will just go there to pick up the car, no one is home. My dad's at work and mom is most likely at the gym."

They grabbed their coats and began the twenty minute drive to the suburb of Rocky River. They pulled up into a driveway that lead up to a huge, red-brick house overlooking Lake Erie. She had told Anthony to stay in the car. She stepped out and then walked to the front door. She rang the doorbell and a woman with short, blond hair opened the door. They hugged, and Lisa went in.

I thought she said that no one would be home now, Anthony thought, as he watched from the car. He waited and waited. It is now 11:30 a.m., and Lisa is still not out of the house. *What is taking her so long? It's been 15 minutes.* Out of boredom, he started looking through the car. A tap on the window frightened him and he jumped in his seat. He looked out of the window and saw Lisa standing with her hands on her hips. *Great,* he thought. He closed the glove compartment, opened the door and stepped out of the car.

"Sorry, I was bored," he said to her apologetically, as he shrugged his shoulders.

"Follow me," she said to him as she walked towards the back of the house and stopped in front of the garage. She opened it up and handed him the keys to a black, 2014 Hummer.

"Wow, you are going to let me drive that?" He was stunned. "Uhhh, maybe we can just go to a used car dealership and we can just get me a beat up car. This is way too much."

"Why do that when this car is paid for and available!" she said as she rolled her eyes. "You take the Hummer. I am going to go home and do some work. How about we meet at Marie's for dinner at about 7 tonight. You do remember where it is, don't you?"

"Yes I do! 45th on St. Clair!" He smiled that sexy smile of his. "It used to be my favorite place. I'm so happy that it's still around! I am going to pay a visit to my mom at the nursing home. And I also want to go and check out the storage where all of the things from the house were taken to. If I'm done early enough, I'll meet you at home and we can ride to the restaurant together." He recalled her phone conversation earlier today. "Are we eating solo tonight?"

"Actually, we will be meeting a couple of good friends of mine there. So I will see you later." She walked away and disappeared into the front of the house.

I can't believe that she is letting me borrow the Hummer. He could never afford such a beauty. His last and only car was a red, 1998 Toyota Corolla. His father bought that car for him when he graduated high school. He didn't have a high paying job, and since he had to pay his college tuition, and rent, he couldn't afford to ever get another one. He carefully backed it out of the garage, passed the house and drove onto the street. *First stop will be the nursing home where his mother lives.*

Chapter 3

Anthony Rozman was born on March 7, 1976 in the Cleveland suburb of Fairview Park. He went to the Fairview Park public schools. After he graduated from high school, he went to Kent State University where he graduated with his master's degree in architecture. It was a 6 year program and he was able to get a job right after graduation. He worked for H&N Architects on 25th and Superior Avenue for 9 years before he was arrested.

His mother was a cashier at a gas station, and his father was a a car salesman. His dad passed away two years ago, and Anthony always regretted not being able to attend the funeral. He wasn't very close to his father, Tom, but he always made sure that Anthony had everything he needed. His dad was of average height with blond hair and blue eyes. Anthony didn't look anything like him. In fact, they didn't have much in common. For instance, his father wasn't into sports like he was. And there was never any bonding with his father. They never went to sporting events, camping, or fishing like all of his friends and their dads did. His mother, Mary, used to work the evening shift so that she could stay at home with Anthony during the day. His mom was a beautiful, tall and slender brown- eyed brunette. During Anthony's second year in prison, his father visited and told him that his mother was suffering from Alzheimer's disease. After Tom died, she became unable to take care of herself, and since there was no family to help, she was put in a nursing home. Anthony had Lisa check in on everything and because he couldn't do anything, he had Lisa assume the Power of Attorney. She was able to sell the house that they lived in, and the money from the sale has been helping to pay for his mom's care. He couldn't wait to see her. Lisa told him that she might not remember him and that was something that he wasn't looking forward to. He studied all that he could on Alzheimer's disease while he was in prison, so he was somewhat prepared for the worst.

He parked the Hummer in the parking lot of the nursing home, and with a bag in hand, he walked in through the glass door. There was a nasty odor that almost made him throw up. It smelled like medicine, alcohol, and urine all combined into one horrible scent. He approached the receptionist and told her that he was here to visit his mom. The short, elderly lady told him that she was in room 205. She pointed him in the right direction, and when he came up to the closed door, he hesitated before going in. He stopped for a minute and then softly knocked on the door. He didn't hear anything so he knocked loudly and then opened the door that led him to the one person he loved more than anything.

He got the chills as he walked into the somewhat cold room. His first sight was of an empty bed. His mom was sitting in a chair, covered in a little blue blanket, looking out the only window. She didn't hear him walk in and continued to stare out at the snowy field and a little frozen pond. He grabbed a chair that was in the corner of the room and took a seat next to her.

"Hi, Mom," he said to her as he gently took her hand and held it. She turned to look at him and smiled. He was surprised at how much she changed. She was no longer the woman he saw last. She looked as she aged beyond her years. Her hair was almost all grey and her face looked skinny and more wrinkled. She wasn't the strong woman he remembered. She was now a frail, sick woman.

"Jerry? I can't believe that you came to see me," she uttered.

"It's Anthony, Mom, not Jerry. I'm your son. Don't you remember?"

"Oh," she said and frowned. "You look so much like Jerry." She turned her head back to the window.

"Are you hungry? I brought you a couple of sandwiches and french fries."

"Did you bring the wine, too? You know the one we used to drink together at the park? Gosh, Jerry, we used to have so much fun together." She started to laugh. "Remember that night when we drank the whole bottle? I don't know how I got home that night, but I remember how upset my father was." She shook her head.

"Mom, it's Anthony!" He was becoming upset even though he knew he shouldn't be. "I am your son. Don't you remember me?" She looked at him for a second and sighed.

"You look so much like Jerry."

They sat in silence for a while and Anthony looked at the clock on the wall. It was time for him to go. He still wanted to go to the storage place to go through some of the things there. He got up and kissed his mom on her head.

"Goodbye, Mom, I'll see you soon," he whispered in her ear and left.

That was a real disappointment. She didn't remember him and he was crushed. He was angry and depressed. He wondered who Jerry was. He didn't remember a Jerry or anyone ever mentioning that name. Now he regretted his father's death even more. He wished that he had some family members whom he could talk with. At least he isn't all alone. He has Lisa and Howard. Maybe they are all he needs.

He had known Howard Filiere since he had graduated from college. Howard, and his partner, Nick, had interviewed him for the job at H&N. Howard is now in his late seventies and is still working hard. He supported Anthony, unlike other people, and even visited him often while he was in prison. Anthony admired Howard more

31

than anyone. Even with Howard's sarcasm, they bonded and became close. They didn't just work together; they went to ballgames, movies, dinner; they did everything Anthony wished that he did with his father. He was supposed to meet Howard on Sunday for brunch and he couldn't wait to talk to him.

He drove to the storage facility and found the compartment that he had been looking for and opened it. There were boxes and boxes piled to the top. It was a 12'x12' area and it was packed. He couldn't even enter it. He took a box out and opened it. It was full of books. *I don't need these*, he thought. *It is going to take me forever to go through all of these boxes.* He grimaces at the thought. He went through five boxes and decided that he had enough. It was almost 4:30. He put the boxes that he went through to the side and marked an 'x' on each one. He locked the door of the storage unit and decided to go home.

He noticed when he parked the car in the garage that Lisa's BMW wasn't there. He went up to the apartment feeling gloomy. He had a crappy day, and he hoped that the night would be better. He at least knew that the food would taste good. He took a shower and dressed. He put on a pair of khaki pants and a blue dress shirt and sat on the couch to wait for Lisa. It was 6 p.m. and Lisa still wasn't home. He leaned back and closed his eyes. He thought about how his life had become such a great big mess and what did he do to deserve it. But mainly, he thought about how his mom had forgotten him.

"Anthony, Anthony," Lisa nudged his shoulder. "Anthony," she said one more time as he finally opened his eyes. "It's 6:45, we have to go."

He wiped his eyes and looked at her. She was wearing a pair of black slacks and a purple dress shirt that was visible through the dark grey coat that she was wearing. Her hair was up in a

messy pony tail. *She looks sexy*, he thought as he got up off the couch and put his coat on.

"You want to drive or shall I?" she cheerfully asked him.

"I will, and let's take the Hummer. I totally love that car!"

He parked the car on the side street and they walked into the restaurant. They were greeted by a waitress at the little bar who told them to have a seat anywhere the like. He followed Lisa who decided on a table by a window. They sat down and were given menus. The waitress took their drink order and Lisa told her that we would wait until her friends arrived. They were a few minutes early and Jo and Bob were still not here. He studied the place a little. It still looked the same as it did. The walls were a different color from before. He remembered it being white, not a light shade of brown. The old style metal ceiling was painted white and the moldings in brown.

"Did you know that the ceiling here is original? It's beautiful," he said as he took a sip of the Pepsi he had ordered.

"It is beautiful. The design is remarkable," she replied. "Here they come," she smiled as she saw Jo and Bob parking their car in front of the restaurant.

He had a great night at Marie's. He had the spaghetti with a brown meat sauce that he thought was remarkable. Lisa had the schnitzel, Jo had the beef goulash and Bob had the spaghetti, as well. He met Lisa's best friend, Jo, and her boyfriend, Bob, who was a lot older than Anthony thought that he would be. Jo is in her forties. She has curly, long brown hair, and beautiful almond shaped eyes. Anthony thought she was cute and very lively. She was interesting and kept the conversation going. Bob was much older then she and was pretty outspoken. He seemed like a great guy who kind of reminded him of Howard. He wasn't sure what Jo was doing with someone that much older than she was, but he guessed that age doesn't matter when it comes to love.

Chapter 4

It was Saturday morning, and this time, Anthony woke up early and decided to make breakfast. He thought that that was the least he could do for Lisa. She bent over backwards for him and he still couldn't figure out why. She didn't even know him or anything about him, and yet she saved him and was able to get him out of prison. On top of all that, she also gave him a place to stay, a new wardrobe, and a car to borrow. *She is a saint!* He put the last of the pancakes on the plate and poured himself a cup of coffee. *This Keurig coffee maker is awesome,* he thought as he took his first sip of the steamy coffee. *Mmm, delicious, I hope the pancakes are just as good.* It has been a long time since he made them or cooked anything at all.

Lisa didn't sleep well last night. She tossed and turned for most of the night. She thought that the dinner went well, and Jo seemed to have hit it off well with Anthony. Lisa was even a little jealous at how well the two of them were interacting. Anthony seemed to like her. He even mentioned that he liked her on their way home last night. Lisa's stomach turned a little when she thought about him and Jo being together. She spent all night trying to figure out her feelings. She didn't know what these feelings were, but she was positive that it wasn't love. She rolled out of bed at about 9:30 am and put on a pair of gray yoga pants and a sweatshirt. After she used the bathroom, she joined Anthony who was standing in the kitchen, eating pancakes and drinking coffee.

"Morning, would you like a cup of coffee and some pancakes?" Anthony asked her.

"Sure, the pancakes look really good. I didn't know that you can cook." She replied.

"I used to all of the time. The pancakes actually taste pretty good considering I haven't cooked anything in the last five years." He handed her a plate and the utensils, as well as the freshly made cup of coffee. "I hope that you don't mind me going through the kitchen." She walked to the refrigerator and took out the cream for her coffee.

"No, I don't mind at all. Thanks for making the breakfast." Lisa smiled as she prepared her coffee to her liking and then poured maple syrup all over the pancakes. "So what have you planned to do today?"

"I was hoping that I can go back to the storage bin. I really want to get that cleared up. There is so much stuff there, though, I need days just to go through all of those boxes. Are you free today? Maybe you can go with me. I can use the extra hand as well as an extra car. I noticed that a few of the boxes have books in them. I can donate them somewhere, so whatever can't fit in mine we can put in yours."

"Sure, I can help you today, but tomorrow you are on your own. I have court on Monday and I still need to go over everything one more time. I like to be well prepared," she answered as she put a piece of pancake in her mouth. The syrup oozed out of the corner of her mouth and she wiped it with a napkin.

"Thank you! You are the best!" he exclaimed with a smile. He cleared the counter and then washed the dishes, as Lisa took another cup of coffee and sat on the couch.

At about noon, they each drove separately to the storage place. Once there, Anthony right away moved the boxes that were marked with an X into the back of the Hummer.

"These are the ones I went through yesterday. They're all books. There used to be a place around here that took them. I think it used to be called Half Price Books. Do you know which place I am talking about?"

"Yes, I do. The place is still around but not at the same location. They moved farther down Lorain. I know exactly where it is. How about I take them there right now while you go through more of the boxes?" She handed him the box of garbage bags that they had grabbed from home and left with the Hummer.

Five down, and like 50 more to go! He grabbed another box and opened it. He went through it and tossed everything in a trash bag. All of these boxes were from his parents' house. His mom apparently kept all of Anthony's school papers, books, and a bunch of notebooks. He didn't even know that she had all of these things. He found all of his sports trophies in one box. He used to play basketball and run track. He was a star athlete and had won many awards. *Should I throw them out too? Maybe I'll ask Lisa what she thinks when she gets back. I really don't have much use for them anymore.* He put them to the side and reached for another box. He wiped the dust off the lid and opened it. Papers, lots and lots of papers. He took a trash bag and set it right next to the box. He went through each of the papers. This box contained all of his report cards, certificates of merit, and the newspaper clippings that mentioned him. *I can't believe my mom kept all of these things.*

"I'm back," Lisa interrupted his thoughts. "I took the books back. Wow! You cleared a lot of boxes! Are all these bags full of stuff to be discarded?"

"I'm afraid so," he sighed. "My mom kept every little keepsake that she could have from me. I even found all of my trophies. I threw all of the papers away, but to tell you the truth, I'm not sure if I should keep the trophies. Would you keep them?"

"I don't know. I never received a trophy for anything. Maybe you should keep them. They represent a good part of your life. It's a nice feeling to know that you have won something. It would be good to one day share that with your children." She smiled at the thought.

"I guess you're right. I have five boxes left including the trophies. Would you mind if I take them back to your place? I can go through them there later. It's 3:00 p.m. and I'm hungry."

"Not a problem. You load up the rest of the boxes, and I will go tell them in the office that they can dispose of the things that are left. I will also tell them that we no longer will need the space."

He loaded up the Hummer with the remaining boxes, and waited for Lisa to come out of the office. He was happy to know that his mom kept all of his things. Even though she couldn't remember his name or who he was yesterday, now he knew that she really loved him.

Chapter 5

Anthony woke up with a smile on his face. It's Sunday, and he gets to have brunch with Howard. He looked forward to seeing him today. He last saw him a few months ago when Howard paid him a visit. He got up and used the bathroom. He put on a pair of dark, navy jeans and a light blue dress shirt. It was 10 a.m. when he made it to the kitchen. He didn't see or hear Lisa walking around, so he thought that she must have still been sleeping. He made himself a cup of coffee and sat down on a stool by the kitchen counter. He noticed The Plain Dealer on the counter and took a few minutes to scan through it. Once he finished his coffee, he headed out the door.

Lisa gotten up early and decided to go to her office. She took her coffee to go and didn't tell Anthony that she was going. She had court on Monday and wanted to go through all of the paperwork so that she could be fully prepared. Her client was supposed to meet her there at 10.

She heard the sound of clicking down the hall and knew that her client would be there soon. Even at fifty, Susan wore high heels.

Susan knocked on the door and walked into Lisa's small office. The office consisted of one large desk with a laptop and two chairs. The walls were beige with brown, vertical stripes. On the wall to the left hung a painting of a light house surrounded by the waves of the ocean. The wall behind Lisa's desk held her credentials in black frames. Three, to be exact. One was her college diploma, one was her law school diploma, and one was a certificate that showed that she passed the bar exam. Her office was simple and neat.

Lisa stood up as Susan neared her desk and extended her hand to greet her. Susan had been married for 13 years and wanted out of her marriage because of her husband's infidelity. They have no kids, so the case wasn't difficult to deal with for Lisa. She didn't like dealing with divorce when kids were involved. No child wants to go through that and she hated their look of sadness when she had to speak with them.

"Susan, how are you?" Lisa asks as Susan takes a seat.

"To tell you the truth, a little nervous. I hope that he agrees to everything so that I can just move on with my life. I gave this man thirteen years of my life and all so that he can do what? Fool around with other women. The first time, I let it slide, but this time no way!" Susan said. "Sorry, I just get so upset when I talk about it."

I feel so bad for her, thank God I never plan on getting married or having children. Who needs to worry about all of these things? My life is perfect just the way it is. I feel horrible for all of the men and women that so often get cheated on. When there are kids involved the divorce is twice as bad. But then again, who wants to be in a loveless marriage? My parents don't love each other, and yet are still together.

"Tomorrow will be a piece of cake. I spoke with his attorney the other day and was informed that he will sign the papers. To sum it all up, you will get the house, you will also keep the Jeep, and on top of that, you will get spousal support until he proves that you no longer need it. All we have to do is go over the fine points, and then sign the papers," Lisa smiled. "Make sure that you are at the courthouse at 8 a.m. I will meet you there in the lobby. We have to all meet in the room at 8:30."

"Okay, I will be there. And thank you so much Lisa. I truly appreciate it," Susan said as she stood up and shook Lisa's hand. "See you tomorrow," and she left the office.

Lisa put all of the paperwork in her folder, then into her briefcase. She put on her coat, and heard someone walk into the room.

"Long time no see, Lisa." It was a voice she recognized.

NO,NO,NO! It can't be. She turned around and was face to face with the only man who ever broke her heart.

Chapter 6

Howard was early and grabbed a table at the corner of this little restaurant so that they could talk in private. The place was practically empty now, but is going to start filling up soon after Sunday mass. He was reading the newspaper when Anthony strolled over to the table.

"Hi, Howard!" Anthony said, delighted to see him. Howard looked up and extended his hand.

"Anthony! So good to see you in regular clothes." Howard laughed. "I do have to tell you, though, I was finally starting to get used to seeing that orange color on you." Anthony grinned. He sure missed Howard's sense of humor. The waitress came over to take their orders and poured each of them a cup of coffee.

"Well? How is everything going? I don't see why you didn't want to stay with me. I know I'm not as good looking as Lisa, but still." Howard said.

"Howard, I told you that I'll be trying to figure out why someone framed me. I care too much for you to get you involved. How do we know that whoever is behind it won't want to come after me. Someone apparently wants to ruin me. And I am going to find out who and why!"

"And how in the hell are you going to do that?"

"I don't know yet. But the first thing that I am going to do tomorrow is go to the police station with Lisa, and I'm going to see if they will reopen the case. I want to find out who actually murdered those women. I'm at least going to get a detective to help me. I plan on doing everything legally. There is no way in hell that I am ever putting on an orange jumpsuit again"

"Are you coming in to work tomorrow?" Howard asked.

"Yes, do I get my old office back? I really appreciate you and Nick giving me the job back. Thanks to you, I at least have a way of starting all over again."

"I told you that I will always be there for you. Did you get to see your mom yet?

47

"Yes, I did. It was horrible. She didn't even know who I was. I think I'll pay her a visit later on tonight. You want to come with me?"

"No, thanks, I plan on watching some basketball tonight."

"I haven't watched a game in years. I don't even know who the players are now."

Howard spent the next 20 minutes discussing the Cleveland Cavs. Anthony couldn't believe that Lebron came back. The team is doing well and it looked like they were going to make it into the playoffs. They finished their breakfast and said their goodbyes. Anthony got into the Hummer and headed back home. He wondered where Lisa went so early this morning. He thought she was still asleep, but when he left, he noticed that her car wasn't in the garage.

Chapter 7

"Rob," Lisa said and tried her best to hide her dismay. "What are you doing here?"

"I was in the neighborhood, and thought I'd stop by."

Huh, you are always in the neighborhood, Lisa thought.

"Well, you saw me, and I need to go,"

"Look, Lisa, I know that you don't want anything to do with me, but I'm worried about you. I don't know how you could let him stay at your place."

How does he know that Anthony is staying with me?

"What I do is my business," Lisa angrily said. "Why do you even care?"

"Because I do. I know that what I have done is horrible, and I am sorry for it. Can we at least go and get a cup of coffee? I'll explain everything then," he pleaded. "Please?"

Lisa thought about it for a minute. She was a sucker for those beautiful blue eyes of his.

"Okay, but I can't stay long." He let her lead the way down the long, tiled hallway.

Lisa first noticed Rob at Anthony's trial. Rob was the lead detective on the case and he was present every day of the trial. The two, however, formally met a couple of years ago when she went to talk to him about the case. As a matter of fact, he even helped to lead her in the right direction. They spent about six months dating and she fell in love. But then all of a sudden, he stopped returning her phone calls and text messages. She never heard from him, and she made sure that she never saw him. She was depressed for about three months, and then worked even harder to free Anthony. Keeping busy helped to not think about him. After nearly three years of not seeing or talking to him, she was curious to find out why he abandoned her.

Back at the Loft, Anthony decided to go through a couple of other boxes that he brought from the storage. He wished that he could find something in there of some use. He put two of the boxes that he looked at in the corner of the room. *More papers of absolutely no use!* He sighed. *Maybe I can go through all of Lisa's papers about the case.* She gave him a huge stack of folders the other day that contained all of the information about the trial and everything that she found about the case afterwards. He took the pile of folders from the dresser in his room and carried them into the livingroom, where he set them on the coffee table. He went to the kitchen and made himself a cup of coffee. He glanced at the time on the microwave. It was 3 p.m. and Lisa still wasn't home. He took his cell phone out of his back pocket and looked to see if he received any messages. No call and no message. He started to worry about her, and decided to message her:

"Hi, I haven't seen you or heard from you today. Is everything okay?"

A few minutes later, which felt like a lifetime to Anthony, Lisa replied "everything is fine I should be there in a few." He took a seat on the couch and grabbed a folder. He was able to look through a couple of documents before Lisa finally arrived.

"Sorry," she said to Anthony, who was relieved to see her, as she plopped down next to him on the couch. "I went to the office early and then I met with a client. I have court tomorrow morning so I wanted to go over some of the details again."

"It must have been a long meeting!" Anthony replied with a little hint of attitude. "To tell you the truth, I was starting to worry about you."

"I apologize, I didn't think that you would worry. I usually don't answer to anyone,"

"I don't mean to put you on the spot," Anthony interrupted, "I just still feel like someone is out to get me. I feel like I'm also putting you in danger. I feel horrible for even being here."

"Anthony," she sighed, "I told you that you don't need to worry about me. I can take care of myself." She started to giggle. "Didn't I tell you that I have a black belt in tae kwon do?"

A little relieved, he smiled and replied, "No, I had no idea. I guess than you can probably kick my ass."

"Probably! So don't do anything that would really upset me," she laughed. "I see you're looking through some files. Any thoughts?"

"I was looking at the files of the three women." He spread the three files on the table. "The only thing that these women have in common with me is that we all hung out at the same bar. I only dated Ashley Wright and she was killed last. You know I felt so bad that she was killed. I liked her a lot. So much so, that I even went to her wake at Zak's Funeral Home. I didn't have enough guts to go into the building so I parked in front of the place across the street and just watched the people enter and leave. I don't get it. I need to investigate their lives to see if there is another common link. As far as I know, these women didn't know each other. That private investigator that you hired did a great job. I just don't recognize any names of the people that these women were involved with."

"We couldn't find a common link either. We have come up with the conclusion that it is someone from your past that did the killings."

"But who?" He looked at her with such puzzled, sad eyes that just for a second she thought that her heart was going to melt.

"You'll figure it out, I know you will." She patted his hand as a comforting gesture. "What would you like to have for dinner tonight? I was thinking we should just order some pizza."

"That's fine with me," Anthony replied, as he gathered up all of the papers and stacked them up on the table. "I think that I'll pay a visit to my mom, though, first. You want to come along?"

"No, not really. I'm not a fan of nursing homes. You go ahead and I will order pizza and have it here at 7." Anthony took the files and put them back in his room. He grabbed his coat and left.

It was early for Lisa to order pizza, so she decided to make herself a cup of coffee and relax a little. She needed some time to process everything that was going on. She thought that helping Anthony get out of prison was going to give her relief but it hasn't. It just made things even worse. Her conscience was killing her, and after talking with Rob today she was even more unsure of what to do. "I think you did enough to help him" Rob had told her earlier.

"It's not like you murdered those women!" *No, I didn't kill them. I just feel like I did. Rob thinks I should just let it go before Anthony finds all of the missing clues. Then we would all be screwed. If I tell Anthony the truth, maybe nothing will happen.* She took a sip out of her cup and swallowed the hot coffee. She had no idea what to make out of the conversation that she had earlier with Rob. When she asked him why he left her high and dry, he apologized and said that he was scared when he realized that he was in love with her. He said that he wanted to concentrate on his career and he didn't want to get seriously involved with anyone. However, Lisa thought that that was all a bunch of lies. She used to trust him and he held her heart in the palm of his hand. What did he do with it? He threw it to the ground and stepped on it.

Chapter 8

Anthony knocked on the door and stepped in to his mother's room. He still couldn't get used to the nasty smell of the place. This time his mom was sleeping in the bed. He quietly grabbed a chair and pulled it next to the bed. He didn't want to disturb her so he sat down and gazed at her. She looked terrible, he thought. She was pasty white, and seemed so frail. He glanced around the room and noticed a vase full of yellow roses on the window pane. *Yellow roses are her favorite, I wonder who brought these*? He walked over to the window. He was hoping there was a card that came with them, but he didn't see one. He crept to the dresser by the bed and opened the first drawer. He started to shuffle through the papers and his mom awoke.

"Who are you? What are you doing?" She screamed. "Help, Help!"

Startled, he jumped back, and in a mode of panic started to back away when a nurse barged in through the door.

"What's going on here?"

"He's trying to steal things! Call the police!" she yelled to the nurse, who seemed to be shaking her head in disbelief.

"It's okay," the nurse walked over to her and grabbed her hand. "This is your son, you don't remember? He was just here the other day."

His mom looked at him and a couple of minutes later uttered, "Oh, Anthony, *She remembers me!* "It's you, I'm so sorry. I was sleeping and I couldn't recognize you." *I can't believe she remembers me!* "Come over here and let me see you. I missed you." He slowly walked over and took a seat on the bed next to her. He clutched her hand and replied, "I missed you, too. You remember, me?"

"Yes, sweetheart, of course I do. I don't think that I could ever forget you." *Oh, mom, you did and you will again.*

"I noticed the flowers, who gave them to you?"

"Oh, that reminds me, I'm supposed to give you something." She sat up and lifted the blue blanket that was covering her. She pulled out an envelope with the word "Anthony" printed on the front. "Someone brought me those beautiful flowers today. They are my favorite." She paused a couple of seconds as she eyed them. "He gave me this envelope and told me to give it to you."

"Who brought it?" Anthony asked as he took the envelope from her frail, left hand.

"The delivery boy. He said that the flowers are for me, and that I need to give this envelope to you."

"Did he tell you who it's from?"

"I don't remember," she replied and lay back down. "I'm tired, will you come again?"

"Yes, I will, soon." She closed her eyes and mumbled something that he didn't quite catch. Anthony opened up the envelope and pulled a card out. To his horror, he read to himself *"STOP DIGGING BEFORE THE GRAVE GETS FULL."* He put the card back in the envelope, kissed his mom on the cheek and quietly stepped out of the room. He stopped at the reception desk and greeted the woman behind the counter.

"Someone, dropped off flowers and a card to my mother today. I would like to know who it was."

"And what is your mother's name and room number?"

"Her name is Mary Rozman, she's in room 205," Anthony answered as he grabbed a pen off the desk and started to tap it against the edge. After a few minutes of looking through the sign in chart, the short, pudgy woman said,

"She didn't have any visitors today. No one signed in to see her." He flung the pen back on the desk and angrily asked,

"How do you just let anyone come in here?" he said realizing that even he was able to just walk in here today and no one noticed.

Stunned at his manner, she retorted, "I am sorry sir, but we are understaffed. The home can't afford to have someone stand at the door and ask for everyone's ID. If you would like, I can give you the number of the supervisor, and you can give them a call."

"Yes, please do." The woman handed him a business card and Anthony stormed out of the nursing home.

He drove straight home all the while checking the mirrors for fear of being followed. He didn't know if he should go to the police or figure it out himself. He parked the car in the garage next to Lisa's and walked towards the elevator. He had this horrible feeling ever since he read the card. He knew it was a threat. Now he knew that he had a big decision to make. He can get on with his life, or he can try to figure it out and risk someone else getting hurt. *If someone else gets killed, can I live with the guilt?*

He entered the apartment and found Lisa sitting on the couch.

"Hi," she said as he sat down next to her. "How was the visit with your mom?"

"The visit was actually good, my mom remembered me for a little bit today. Someone dropped off flowers for her today, and this for me." He handed her the envelope. She opened it up and pulled out the card.

"Oh my God!" she exclaimed. "Did you find out who delivered it?"

"No one signed in to see her today. That nursing home just lets anyone go in. Whoever it was knew her room number. He even knew what her favorite flowers are," Anthony replied in disgust.

"I think that I'll sleep on it tonight, and I go to the police station tomorrow. Maybe someone there can help me out."

"I think that would be a wise decision. I am going to order pizza," Lisa said as she grabbed her phone and entered the number. She ordered one medium pepperoni, and one with chicken and pineapple. "The pizza will be here in about 20 minutes." She stood up and walked to the kitchen. "I am going to pour myself a glass of wine. Would you like one as well?"

"Sure, why not." He watched her pour the red wine into two glasses. "Are you scared?"

"No, not really," she lied. She was scared but not for the same reason that Anthony was thinking. The pizza arrived right on time. They ate the pizza and finished off the bottle of wine. After a long comfortable silence, Lisa spoke up. "Are you scared?"

"Good question, Lisa." He started to laugh hysterically. "I just spent 5 years in a maximum security prison. I don't think I'm scared of much anymore. However, it does freak me out knowing that because of something that I am doing, someone else that I care about could die. I don't know if I can live with that guilt if it happens, to tell you the truth."

"I know exactly what you mean." *I am still living with that guilt.* "I think that I'm going to call it a night. I have to be in court by eight. And you are starting work tomorrow, right?" She stood up and took the glasses to the kitchen and put them in the sink. Anthony, who was right behind her, set the pizza box on the kitchen counter.

"Yes, I am. I told Howard that I'll be there."

"If you decide to go to the police let me know. I can meet you there at noon." He walked close to the sink where Lisa was still standing.

"Tell me again why you have been so nice to me. You saved my life, and I want to know why." She had no idea what to say; she wasn't ready to answer that particular question yet. He leaned in and whispered in her ear, "why, Lisa, tell me, please." He started to nibble on her right earlobe. He breathed in the sweet scent of her perfume, and whispered again, "tell me." He kissed her cheek and slowly moved his lips closer to her mouth. All of a sudden, he stepped back and held her chin and moved her head up so she was looking into his eyes. "Why, Lisa?" He asked her again. Her face was flush and he wasn't sure if it was him or the wine that made it so.

"I told you, I just wanted to help." She managed to smile even though she was shocked and confused by his actions. "I think I should go to bed now. I think that bottle of wine got to the both of us. I need to be in court early, and you are going to work as well." Anthony nodded and Lisa walked right by him.

After she used the bathroom she yelled out goodnight to Anthony, who was still in the kitchen leaning over the counter, and went to her bedroom. As she lay in her bed she closed her eyes and replayed the scene that just occurred in the kitchen. She felt a surge of electricity go through her whole body when he touched her. She wondered if he felt that, too. She rolled her eyes at herself. She knew

Anthony hasn't been with a woman in years. She also knew that she wasn't his "type". *It must have been the wine.* She was exhausted from all of the things that happened today and soon fell asleep.

Anthony stayed up a little bit longer. He stayed in the kitchen, leaning over the counter, with his ankles crossed and his head in his hands, he thought about Lisa. *She has no idea of how pretty she is. She is one of the most beautiful women that I have ever met. She is hiding something from me though, that I know. But what? And why won't she just tell me?*

Chapter 9

Anthony woke up fairly early hoping that he could make some coffee and toast for Lisa. But when he stepped into the kitchen, Lisa was already sitting at the counter with a cup of coffee in hand. She wore a black pencil skirt that came right at the knee, and a dark grey dress shirt. Her hair was tied in a low ponytail and looked darker today than yesterday. He wondered if she colored it and how come he didn't notice it last night. She wore her glasses with thick black frames and was looking over a piece of paper which Anthony assumed were the notes for the trial that she had today.

"Good morning," Anthony said as he passed by her.

"Good morning." Lisa didn't look up. She was still embarrassed from last night and couldn't look at him this morning.

"Do you want some more coffee?" Anthony asked as he brewed himself one. "Are you hungry? I'm going to pop in some toast, I can make you some."

"No thanks. I want to get to the courthouse early."

"Okay. Did you want to meet up for lunch? I want to go to the police station to show them the card I received. I want to see if they would reopen the case. Obviously, the murderer is still out there."

"I'm not sure how long I'll be. If I get out early, I'll text you. I would like to go with you." She needed to watch his every move. She grabbed the files that were on the counter and put them in her briefcase. She walked to the front door and took her coat off the rack and put it on. All the while, Anthony drank his coffee and watched her every move. He thought she looked hot as hell this morning.

He was greeted at work by Nick, who led him back to his old office.

"Welcome back," Nick said as Anthony sat down at his old desk. "We haven't changed

a thing since you left, besides a couple of new people we hired. If you need anything just come and get me, you know where I will be. There are a few projects that we are doing and you have all the files for them on your desk. So look through them and start sketching some ideas. And, so you know, Howard called and is running a little late."

"Thank you, Nick. I won't be a disappointment again."

"Son, you were never a disappointment," Nick said.

Anthony looked through his desk drawers and found that they were completely empty. He should have known they would be. The police confiscated everything that was in the office the day that they arrested him. He set his eyes on a box that was on the floor in the corner of the room. He got up to see what it was. He lifted the box and set it on top of his desk. As he was getting ready to open it, he heard someone step into the room and say loudly,

"I see you found it." Howard walked in and stood beside him. "Someone dropped it off earlier this morning. Nick said the guy was here waiting for someone to unlock the door. Come on, open it." Anthony opened the flaps of the box and peeked in. He took out a white envelope with his name on it. His heart started to race as he remembered the card from yesterday.

"That's all?! Why in the heck would someone deliver such a big box with one little envelope!" Howard exclaimed and shook his head.

"Uhh, I think I'll open it later," he said to Howard, not wanting to alarm him. To switch the subject, Anthony asked, "do you have a notebook I could borrow? I didn't bring anything to work with me. I had some ideas for a couple of projects and I wanted to write them down before I forget."

"Well good for you!" Howard patted him on the shoulder. "Already back at work! You can't get any work done with an empty desk." He dug into the back pocket of his suit pants and took out his wallet. "Here is my Visa card. You can buy everything that you need with it."

"Thank you, Howard. I don't know what I would do without you. I promise to pay you back as soon as I can."

"Please," Howard replied, "you don't have to do that. You know that you are like a son to me. This is a welcome home present for you." He put his hand on Anthony's shoulder again and slightly rubbed it. "Now, do as I say, and I will see you in here tomorrow morning at 8." Howard left the room as Anthony exclaimed,

"You got it!" He put his black coat on. It is 10 a.m. so he has a couple of hours to run to the store and get the last few things he needed before he was to meet up with Lisa. Howard has been very generous to him over the years that he has known him. He is going to have to do more than just pay him back the money. He grabbed the box off the desk and left.

He noticed, as he waited to get off the elevator, that the box was getting heavier by the second. *I wonder what's in here. I just hope that whatever it is, it isn't another threat.* Finally, the elevator stopped at the garage level and he walked out along with a couple of other people. He felt the cold wind on his face as he neared the Hummer. He opened the passenger side door and put the box on the seat. He quickly walked to the driver's side all the while looking all around to make sure no one was following him.

He put the keys in the ignition and started the car. He made sure the doors were locked before he reached for the box. Sweat dripped down his forehead as he slowly opened the two flaps of the box and once again looked in. Red tissue paper was on top and he slowly took out the pieces one by one. At the bottom of the box was a black, hard case. It looked like the flute case he used to have in grade school. He played the flute for one year before his mother let him quit. He couldn't stand the instrument and the other boys in the class made fun of him for playing it. He pulled out the case and the envelope. With his adrenaline pumping and face full of sweat, he clicked open the case. It held a knife. It looked like the same knife that was used to kill all three of the women. He closed the case and set it on the seat next to him and carefully opened the envelope. He slowly pulled out the card and read "REMEMBER THIS? DON'T MAKE ME USE IT" "Christ," he mumbled as he slid the card back in the envelope. *What am I supposed to do? Should I go to the police with this? How does this person even know what I am doing?* He wiped his forehead with his sleeve and pulled out his cell phone. It was almost eleven. He sent Lisa a text message to let her know that he was ready whenever she was. *I don't understand why someone is torturing me. If they hate me so much then why not just kill me.*

He started the Hummer and decided to go to the office supply store first. He wanted to please Howard more than anything, so he wanted to be ready to work tomorrow. He missed designing. He did a lot of sketching while he was in prison but no designing. He was depressed and couldn't bring himself to do an actual blueprint of anything. All that did was remind him of the good life that he had, and surely missed. He was glad that he at least kept up the practice of drawing, because his hope of getting out one day came true.

Chapter 10

Lisa finally came out of the courtroom as happy as she could be. Her client received everything that she asked for, and Lisa was able to put away one more win. It was 11:45 a.m. when she looked at her phone and saw that she had a few text messages. The first one was from Jo, asking her how her day was and if she wanted to meet up for coffee. The second one was from Rob, asking how she was. And the third one was from Anthony. She texted Anthony back, letting him know that she was done. And Jo, to let her know when they should meet. She walked to her car that was parked in a garage and quickly turned it on to warm up. It was freezing outside. She looked at her phone and Anthony had replied. "I am buying some things that I need for work, I might be done in an hour or so. " *Perfect* she thought to herself and texted Jo back. "I can meet you at the cafe in fifteen." She saw Jo's reply and drove out of the garage and onto the street. She parked by the cafe and saw Jo sitting at a table.

"Hey," Lisa said, as she sat in a chair across from her. "How are you?"

"I'm going nuts!" she said. "My boss wants me to do like a million things, and on top of work issues I have the family driving me nuts. How are you? How are things with Anthony?"

"To tell you the truth I'm going to cave and tell him everything I know! I was so close last night. We almost kissed! There is something about him that makes my heart skip a beat."

"He is totally hot! And he seems so much nicer than you know who."

"Speaking of him," Lisa took out her phone and showed her the message that Rob had sent her. "I didn't reply back yet. I don't even know what to say. It's one thing to break up with

someone, but it's a totally different thing just ignoring another person. He made me feel like crap!"

"You saw him the other day, any feelings come back?"

"Unfortunately, yes. He just looks so good. I don't understand how things can be going so well and then all of a sudden he flat out disappeared. I was imagining our kids for God's sake." Lisa started to laugh. "Can you believe that one?" Her phone beeped and it was a text from Anthony. "I'll have him pick me up here. He wants to go to the police station to report that card that he received. I think I know who sent it, but I am not going to say anything. I really want to stay out of it." She took a sip of coffee that Jo had ordered for her. "This coffee is delicious. I'm kind of hungry, did you eat?"

"Nope, I waited for you to order the food. I just got here a few minutes before you." Jo flagged down the waitress. "I want the chicken wrap," she said as the waitress wrote it down.

"How about you?" the waitress turned toward Lisa and asked.

"I think that I'll have the same, thank you," Lisa responded as she handed the menu back to the waitress.

"Will you be needing anything else?"

"Just some more coffee," Jo and Lisa said in unison, and laughed.

At the office supply store, Anthony was able to buy everything he needed. He even bought a new laptop with the programs that he needed for work. He quickly got out of the store with a bunch of bags and put them in the back of the Hummer. He knew he didn't miss the cold weather. He was feeling pretty nervous so he walked around the car to make sure there was nothing wrong with it. He tried to be alert while in the store, but didn't notice anyone following him around. He got in and did the sign of the cross before he turned the ignition on. He couldn't wait to meet up with Lisa so that she could go with him to the police station. It took him about twenty minutes to get to the cafe. He was pretty surprised to see that her friend was there as well when he walked in.

"Hello, ladies," he said as he took a seat.

"You remember my friend Jo, right?" Lisa asks.

"How could I forget," Anthony smiled, "How are you?"

"I'm fine, thank you for asking. How are you? Are you adjusting fine, since you have been out?"

"I am adjusting pretty well. I have great friends." He looked at Lisa and winked. With red cheeks from blushing, not from being cold, Lisa stood up and said, "We should get going, Anthony."

"Yes, we should." Anthony rose up. "It was nice to see you again. Maybe we can all have dinner again real soon, and please give my regards to Bob."

"It is great to see you, too" Jo replied. "And I will talk to you later, Lisa." Lisa nodded and waved goodbye as she followed Anthony out of the cafe.

Once they got into the Hummer, Anthony started to cry out,

"I go into the office and there was a package there for me. didn't want to open it in front of Howard, so I waited until I got into the car. You won't believe what was in it!" He pulled out the box from the back. "It's a knife that looks exactly like the one that was used to kill those women. Don't touch it!" he yelled at her as she was about to grab it from him.

"Good thinking," she replied. "The fewer fingerprints, the better."

"There was another card in the package as well."

"What did it say?"

"It read, "REMEMBER THIS? DON'T MAKE ME USE IT." We are going to go to the police station right now."

"Do you have the other card as well?" Lisa asked.

"Yes I do," he replied as he pulled out into the traffic.

The police station was full and there was a line that formed by the front desk. Two police officers were assisting people. There were a couple of rows of chairs that were all occupied.

"There sure are a lot of people here today," Anthony said as they stood in line.

There were two more people ahead of them. As they waited patiently for their turn at the desk, Lisa thought, *I hope that I don't run into Rob.* She tried to hide herself between Anthony and a man who stood behind her. She hoped that they weren't here too long. Running into Rob would be a nightmare.

Anthony moved forward and is greeted by a uniform police officer.

"Hi," the policeman said as Anthony approached the desk. "How can I help you?

"I was hoping that I could talk with someone about the Anthony Rozman case."

"What is your name, and why is it that you need to talk with someone?" he asked as he typed something on the computer in front of him.

"My name is Anthony Rozman." The police officer stopped typing and looked up at him.

"You're Anthony Rozman?" he asked, surprised. He remembered the case which was all over the news for weeks, but he hadn't heard anything of it since. "Do you have an ID?"

"No, I don't," Anthony replied. "I just got out of prison. I didn't go to the license bureau yet." *I am an idiot. I should have known that I would need that!*

"Why don't you have a seat and I'll see if anyone is here that could assist you," the officer said as he pointed to the waiting area.

"Man, Lisa, I can't believe that I didn't even think about that. I need a license."

"Maybe we can go if there is still enough time today," Lisa replied as they stood in a corner of the room and waited.

They fortunately didn't wait that long. A short, stocky man dressed in a black suit walked over to them. His badge was pinned to his belt and his gun was strapped to the holster on his hip.

"Hello," he said to the both of them. "I'm Detective Frank Bova. Why don't we walk over to my office and have a talk. What's in the box?" he asked as he eyed the package that Anthony was tightly gripping.

"That's what I wanted to talk with someone about. Someone has been sending me threats. This is what I received so far," Anthony replied.

"I see, follow me, please." He steered them through another door and down a narrow hallway. He entered a little room that Anthony assumed was the detective's office. *I think my prison cell was bigger than this room*, Anthony thought as he followed the detective in.

"Have a seat," the detective told them, as they each took a seat on a wooden chair, "So you are Anthony Rozman, and who are you?" he asked as he looked at Lisa.

"I'm his attorney, Lisa Furrow," she replied and extended her hand to shake the detective's.

"I have been assigned to re-open the case. Obviously, you were set free." The detective looked back at Anthony. "I'll be going through everything and starting all over. I am actually glad that you stopped by. I was going to give you each a call. Mr. Rozman, …"

"Anthony, please."

The detective nodded and continued.

"Anthony, you said that you have been getting threats?"

"Yes." He put the package on the desk.

The detective put on a pair of latex gloves which he pulled out of his pocket and opened up the box. He pulled out a couple of envelopes and the black case. He studied everything and took notes as Anthony told him when and how these things were delivered.

"I am going to get this all examined," Detective Frank said. "It could be anyone who sent this to you. I could see how any member of the victims' families would want to take revenge for their loved one."

"That could be, but I doubt it. I think that whoever framed me is the one threatening me."

"If I find out anything, you'll be the first to know." The detective handed them each a piece of paper and told them to write down their phone numbers. He then gave them each a card of his and told them that if anything else turned up to give him a call right away.

They walk out of the office and down the hall, when someone grabbed Lisa's elbow.

"Hey," Rob whispered to her. "What are you doing here?" Anthony didn't notice that Lisa was stopped and continued to walk forward.

"Something came up, and I came here with Anthony. We just talked with the detective that is working on the case."

"They're reopening it?" Rob asked, surprised that someone is working on the case this soon. The police department has many cold cases that have been on the waiting list. He wondered how come this one seemed to be such a priority. He is going to have to have a chat with Frank. He wondered how come no one told him about the reopening of the case.

"Yes, I need to go," she replied and walked off as fast as she could before Anthony noticed that she wasn't right behind him. As she neared him she stumbled and ran right into him.

"Sorry," she smiled, "I lost my balance." For a few seconds she thought that she was lucky that Anthony didn't see her with Rob, but then he asked her, "Who was that?"

"Just a friend," she answered, and that was all that was said as they reached the car. He turned on the car and looked over at Lisa who was fidgeting with her hands.

"I am going to drop you off at your car and then I'll go get my license. I don't know when I will be back later. I plan on visiting my mom."

"Okay," she said as she heard her phone vibrating. She took a look at it. Text from Rob.

"It's Jo. She wants to meet up later. I have a couple of cases coming up, though, so I think that I'll just go home and work on those later."

Without another word, he dropped her off by the car and took off.

She must think I am that stupid! I know very well who that man was. How could I forget?! It was because of him that my life was turned upside down. He was upset and didn't realize that he had just passed through a red light and almost caused an accident. He looked through the rearview mirror hoping that a cop wasn't behind him. He went on the freeway and drove the speed limit all the way to the North Olmsted license bureau. Once there, he had to take the written test, as well as the driving portion to get his license. Luckily, he had his social security card with him. It took a while but he did it. It was almost 6 p.m. when he left the bureau. He stopped at Olive Garden and bought dinner for his mom and himself.

Chapter 11

His mom was sitting in the bed and wide awake when he walked into the room.

"Hi, Mom." He sat down on a chair by her bed. His mom didn't say a word. "Are you hungry? Did you eat dinner yet?" He took the dinners out of the bag and opened one up for her and put it on a bedside table. He put the tray over her lap. He opened up the plastic silverware and handed her a fork. She took the fork from him and stuck it into the pasta bowl. He grabbed the other container and started to wolf his down. He was hungry. When he looked up, he noticed that his mom wasn't eating.

"You aren't hungry?"

"No, not really. Thank you for bringing it to me, Jerry. I appreciate it. Just seeing you makes me happy," she replied as she watched him eat. "We used to have so much fun together!" She smiled and closed her eyes as she thought about Jerry and her past.

"Yes, Mom, we sure did!" He finished all of his pasta and put the empty container back into the bag that it came in. "You don't want to eat anymore?" She shook her head and he disposed of the remains of her dinner.

She watched him put the bag in the white trash can in the corner of the room.

"How come you left me?" she asked him all of a sudden as she lay back on her bed.

"I had to, Mom," he replied as he sat back down on the chair.

"Why do you keep calling me mom?" she asked with a puzzled expression.

"What do you mean? Don't you know who I am?" She looked at him and didn't answer. "It's Anthony, your son! Do you know, now?"

"Ahh, yes, Anthony. You became such a wonderful young man. You look just like your father. You remind me so much of him." She smiled and closed her eyes. Before Anthony was able to say anything else, his mother was sound asleep.

He left the nursing home soon after, and not wanting to go home right away, he drove around for a couple of hours. He drove by his old high school, the church that he used to attend, and the park where he used to play. Absolutely nothing has changed and he was glad. He decided that on Sunday he would go to Mass. He spent the last five years in prison reading the Bible and praying. God gave him hope and peace. If he learned anything the last few years it was that his faith in God grew stronger.

As he drove around some more, he thought about the events that had occurred since he had got out. Nothing made any sense. He didn't understand why Lisa has been so generous. She didn't owe him anything, so why is she helping him? Why was that cop talking to her today? Why did she refer to him as "just a friend"? All of these questions he has for her, and one of these days he is going to corner her and make her answer all of them. He hasn't really been digging into anything yet and someone is threatening him. If he could only figure out who and why. *What have I ever done to someone? Why does someone want to keep ruining me? Isn't*

spending five years in hell good enough? I didn't even kill these

women! Then he thought about his mom. He didn't understand why

she kept insisting that he looked like his father. There wasn't a

resemblance between either of them. *And who in the hell is Jerry?*

He drove the car into the garage and parked it. Instead of

taking the elevator up to the apartment he decided to take the stairs.

He needed to get some exercise. It's been a few days since he was

last at a gym. Lisa had shown him one in the building that he could

use, but he hasn't been in it yet. It was 10 p.m., and he walked into

an empty place. He knew that Lisa was home because he saw her car

in the garage. He figured that she was in bed sleeping. He made

himself a cup of coffee and took it to his bedroom. He put the cup on

the nightstand and changed. He carefully took off his tie not wanting

to ruin it. He always had a problem making that knot. It took him

twenty minutes to put on the tie this morning, and he wasn't going to

make a repeat of that the next day. He hung up the slacks and dress

shirt and put them away in the closet. He grabbed a t-shirt and sweatpants and put them on. He was planning on doing a lot of work tonight and he wanted to be comfortable.

He grabbed the box that had all of those papers from the storage bin and plopped it on the bed. *I am missing something and I will find out what!* He looked at every paper, through every envelope that was in there and still didn't find it. He looked at the stack of files that were on the desk, and got those, too. He searched every folder and still didn't find it. *I don't get it! Mom kept everything, but I can't find my birth certificate. It has to be somewhere, I thought I saw it the other day.* It was nearing 2 a.m. and, feeling distraught, he put all the papers away and decided to go to sleep.

That night he had the most vivid dream. He dreamt that he was driving up St. Clair. He looked to the right and saw Mihelin Travel. He was nearing his favorite restaurant. It was dark out and when he looked at the clock on the dashboard it read 1 a.m. He passed by Marie's Restaurant and kept driving. He stopped and parked across Zak's Funeral home. It was light as day now. He sat in the car and stared at the entrance of the funeral home. They must have had a wake because a lot of people were going in and out. He saw Lisa walking up to the entrance, where she stood next to one of the white pillars. Anthony didn't move, he stayed in the car and watched. A man approached Lisa and kissed her on the cheek. He didn't recognize him. He was much taller than she. He had light brown hair that was spiked on top and he wore a pair of black pants and a blue dress shirt. They talked for a few minutes and then parted. Lisa walked inside the funeral home and the man walked across the street and stood in front of Anthony's car. The man stopped and stared at him through the windshield and Anthony froze. It was as if he was looking in the mirror. *Is that me?* The man tapped the hood with the palm of his right hand, and Anthony woke up drenched in sweat.

The alarm on his phone was ringing and he pressed the off button. He stretched out his arms and wished he could just lie in bed today. But he had to go to work. He wasn't going to be a disappointment to Howard. He got dressed and went to the bathroom. He walked over to the kitchen and made the coffee. He wasn't hungry so he didn't think about breakfast. As the pot of coffee was almost ready, Lisa walked into the kitchen.

"Good morning," she said to Anthony. "Did you sleep well?"

"Morning. Fairly well," he replied. "You went to bed pretty early."

"Yes, I did. I was so tired yesterday." She poured herself a cup of coffee. "Did you want any breakfast?"

"No, thanks. I'm really not hungry this morning, and I want to get to work early." He poured himself coffee in a cup and closed it with a lid. "I'll see you later."

He was nice and early when he walked into work. The security guard let him in and he turned on the lights to the offices. There was a desk in the middle of the room but no one was here yet. He walked around the desk and straight into his office. He turned on the lights and took the things that he bought yesterday out of the bags. Once he had everything organized, he started to go through the files that were left on the desk. He started to write down some ideas in a notebook when Howard walked into the office.

"Good morning," Howard said.

"Good morning! I beat you in today. Does that mean you got lunch?" That's how they used to do it. Whoever came to the office first didn't have to pay for his lunch that day.

"It appears as if I do." Howard started to laugh and Anthony joined in. "Shall I buy us dinner tonight as well?"

"Maybe, I'll let you know," Anthony responded, as Howard started to walk out of the office. At the doorway, Howard turned around and said,

"I'll get you before lunch, I am looking forward to hearing some of the ideas you have for our big project."

Anthony put himself to work. He had so many ideas for the new hotel downtown. As he jotted down the plans, he envisioned the outcome for every idea. He couldn't wait to show his sketches to Nick and Howard. At noon, Howard and Anthony, as well as Nick, went to have lunch. There, Anthony told them about his plans, and he felt confident. When they went back to the offices, Anthony flipped open the computer and started to draw up some plans on Auto-Cad.

It was 5 p.m. when Nick walked into his office.

"You're still here!" Nick said surprised. "I am about to head out, Howard will lock up. Your ideas for the project were great today. I'm glad you're back with us. Have a good night."

"Thanks, Nick. I will head out shortly, too." He packed up all of his things and put them in his computer case. He was feeling pretty proud of himself. He accomplished a lot today and he was pleased with the outcome of one of the designs that he had drawn up on the computer. He said goodnight to Howard and left.

When he got back to the apartment, he noticed that Lisa's car wasn't in the garage and opted to once again take the stairs. *I'll have to check out that gym in this building*, he thought, as he unlocked the door to the apartment. He walked in and hung up his coat on the rack by the door and went straight to the kitchen. He needed some coffee. It was 6 p.m. and he wondered if Lisa was going to come home soon. As he waited for the coffee, he decided to text her. His phone beeped a few seconds later. A message from Lisa. "Will be home late so have dinner without me, sorry, working on a case." He didn't text her back and wondered if he should call Howard for dinner. He really didn't feel like cooking and didn't feel like being social tonight. He took his cup of coffee, and went to the living room. He turned on the TV and searched the guide. He wasn't into TV. He didn't watch it in prison. He thought he spent his time there wisely, hoping for a future.

As he drank his coffee, he thought about Lisa and her behavior the last couple of days. He felt that she was avoiding him, and he wondered if it was because he made a pass at her the other night. He couldn't help himself, he thought, she is hot. He smiled as he thought about how she blushed when he kissed her. His thoughts were interrupted by his phone ringing. He answered,

"Hello?"

"Mr. Rozman?" a man asked him.

"Yes, what can I help you with?"

"This is Detective Frank, just wanted to check in with you," Detective Frank hasn't ruled out Anthony as the killer, and thus wanted to keep track of his every move. "There were no fingerprints other than yours on the items that I took from you," he said to him. "So, back to square one." *Unless he's sending them to himself so that we think he didn't commit the crimes. He knows that he got out of prison on a technicality which is why the case has reopened.* "Has anything happened in the meantime?"

"No, I'll give you a call if it does. You have a great night." Anthony hung up the phone. He wondered if the evidence points to him, if he would end up going back to prison. I got out because the eyewitness lied and the testimony was ruled out. The police have the knife that was used in the killings along with a piece of my hair that they found by it. The eyewitness testimony was what did it. He needs to get cracking on this if he wants to move on with his life. He has been out for almost two weeks and nothing is going his way. He doesn't even know anyone who could help him. Lisa seemed evasive, and Howard, he wants out of it. He doesn't have any other friends, or even family that he can count on.

He was getting hungry now as he looked to see what time it was. It was almost eight. He went to the kitchen and opened up the fridge. He took out some ham, cheese, and mayo and made himself a sandwich with the wheat bread he found in the cupboard. At about 8:30, and still no sign of Lisa, he decided to take a shower and go to bed. Tomorrow will be a busy day.

Chapter 12

He woke up early because he wanted to catch Lisa this morning. He put on a pot of coffee, and decided to make some French toast for breakfast. He was almost finished when Lisa walked in.

"Good morning, Anthony, how are you?" she asked him as she sat down on a stool by the kitchen counter.

"Good morning. Sleep well?" He poured her a cup of coffee and handed it to her along with a plate with a couple of slices of French toast.

"Thank you," she said, as she grabbed the maple syrup that was already on the counter and poured it on her plate. "This is delicious!" she said, after her first bite.

"You've been working a lot the last couple of days, huh?" he asked her. "Big case?"

"I have a couple of them that I am working on. I have been busy. I actually hired an assistant yesterday. I am hoping that she takes some of the load off. How are you doing at work?"

"I'm doing great." Anthony smiled. "We have a couple of big projects we are working on, and I have some great ideas. I missed it all." He sighed as he recalled the last five years he missed out on. "Do you want to join me for dinner, tonight?"

"Sure," she answered, "anywhere in particular you want to go?"

"You decide. Why don't you invite your friend Jo as well?"

"I'll call her later and will see with her," she replied, and wondered why he wanted Jo to come along again. *Maybe he really likes her*. She cringed at the thought. "I should get going," she said, as she moved her empty plate to the side. "Thanks again for breakfast. I"ll text you later about dinner." She grabbed her coat and left.

Anthony left soon after, and went to work. Instead of going to lunch, he decided to get a copy of his birth certificate. He was on the first floor in City Hall, and luckily there wasn't a long line ahead of him. He filled out a piece of paper and as he stood and waited, someone approached him.

"Hi, Anthony," she said. He turned around and saw a real cute brunette looking up at him.

"Hi, Jo. What are you doing here?" he asked, surprised to see her.

"I was going to ask you the same thing," she giggled. "I'm working on a story and needed to pick up some documents from here," she replied, "and you?"

"To tell you the truth, I'm picking up a copy of my birth certificate. I can't find mine. I was surprised they gave me my driver's license the other day without it."

"You're up," Jo said as the person in front of Anthony was finished.

He walked up to the counter with the piece of paper he had filled out earlier requesting his birth certificate. The pudgy woman took his paper, his social security card, and the money for the fee and disappeared to the back of the room. He turned around to speak with Jo but she wasn't there. *I wonder where she went? That's weird. I thought that she needed something for work.* A few minutes later, the woman behind the counter reappeared and slipped him an envelope and a copy of his birth certificate through the little slot in the glass partition.

"Thank you," he said as he grabbed the papers. On his way out of the room, he spotted Jo in the hall. He walked up to her, told her to have a great day and that he hoped to see her later, and then left the building.

As he approached his car that was parked on the street, he noticed something odd. The driver's side window was smashed. As he peered through the broken glass, he eyed a note on the seat, written in red ink, "I WARNED YOU!"

"Christ," he mumbled to himself. He called the detective but he didn't answer so Anthony left him a message. He then called the main police department. After waiting a few minutes, a police car came up to the scene.

Two police officers stepped out of their car and walked over to where Anthony was standing. Anthony, who was trembling, answered their questions and one of them scribbled everything that was said in his notebook. Meanwhile, another patrol car showed up. The woman stepped out of the car with what seemed to be a tool kit. She greeted everyone and proceeded to take fingerprints off the car.

"I'm writing a police report. And we will take the note as evidence. You said that a Detective Frank should be made aware of this?"

"Yes. Someone has been threatening me. This isn't the first threat that I received. Detective Frank Bova is working on the case. I called him but he didn't call me back yet." His shaking hands looked through his wallet and pulled out the detective's card. "Here is his card." He handed it to the officer.

"Bova," the officer said to the other officer who was writing everything down. "We have all the information we need. I'll make sure that Bova sees the report and that he gets the note." He flashed the note that was now in a plastic bag. "If we have any other questions or issues, we will give you a call. Patty will finish checking for the fingerprints and then you can be on your way." The two officers chatted a little with Patty and left. A few minutes later, Patty said,

"All done!" She packed everything away, shook Anthony's hand and drove away.

What am I going to do now? he thought, as he wiped away with a brush the glass that was left on the seat. *Should I call Lisa? I really don't want to freak her out with this. Maybe I can get the window fixed before tonight and she won't see it. She doesn't need to know about it.* He googled auto mechanics on his phone. *Yes! that place is still around. I hope that they can fix it for me right away.* Domestic and Foreign Auto Body, Inc. used to work on his old car. They were always fast and reasonable. Anthony did the sign of the cross and turned on the ignition. He was afraid that the car was going to explode with him in it.

"PHEW," he breathed out. "I made it." He looked in his rearview mirror to see if anyone was behind him. Whoever put that note on the car seemed to know his every move. He didn't tell anyone, not even Lisa, that he was going there today. *Is Jo following me? Why?* He slowly started the short drive to the mechanics.

He was greeted by a lovely woman, Donna, who told him that the car would be ready by 5 p.m. She gave him keys to a car that Anthony could use in the meanwhile.

"Thank you, very much," Anthony said to Donna. "I'll be back at five to pick up the Hummer."

"No problem, sweetheart," she said with a European accent.

When he stepped into his work office Howard, seated at his desk, greeted him.

"Where did you go to lunch today?" he asked.

"Nowhere," Anthony replied. "I took a little drive out to clear my thoughts."

"Anything you want to talk about?"

"Nope. Just trying to move on with my life. I thought it was going to be easy to adjust back to civilization. But it isn't as easy as I thought."

"You just need some time. Maybe you shouldn't have started to work right away. If you need any time off, just let me know."

"All I have is work, Howard. This was what I was looking forward to. You know how much I enjoy this. If anything, the work has helped me not to think about anything else going on."

Howard slowly stood up.

"Okay, then I will let you get back to it."

At 5 p.m. Anthony left the building all the while watching his back. He didn't notice anyone following him. He drove to the mechanics to pick up the Hummer. After he paid for the service, he decided to go to the police station to see Detective Frank. He wondered why he hadn't called him back. When he walked into the station he noticed a long line again. *Damn it. Is this place ever not busy?* He sneaked passed the line and into a narrow hallway. He remembered where the detective's office was. The door was open

104

and Detective Frank wasn't in sight. *Now what? Should I sit and wait?* He sat on a chair in the office and took out his phone. Once again he called the detective, and once again, there was no answer.

"Can I help you?" Anthony looked up and saw Rob Tucker standing in the office next to him.

"I have been trying to get ahold of detective Frank and he isn't picking up his phone. I left a couple of messages and he didn't call me back yet. So I figured I would come here to see him." This officer gave him the chills and he despised him for not doing a better job with the first investigation.

"He obviously isn't here. Was there an emergency? Do you need something that I can help you with?" *Yeah, like how you helped me out the first time,* Anthony thought as he stood up.

"No, not really. If you see him, though, please tell him that I stopped by."

"I'll let him know. Mr. Rozman, I hope that there aren't any hurt feelings. I was just doing my job," Rob said that with as much sincerity as he could muster up. He offered his hand and Anthony shook it. "And please give my regards to Lisa."

Anthony, now even more agitated, left the police station. He stepped into the Hummer and called Lisa to see if and where they would be meeting for dinner. After no answer he threw the phone on the passenger seat and blurted out loud, "Why in the hell do people have phones and then don't pick them up when someone calls them?!!" He turned on the car and went home. He picked up the mail that was in the lobby for the two of them, and this time waited for the elevator. He got off on his floor and as he approached the apartment, the door was open. He cautiously entered. He didn't see or hear anyone. The place didn't look like it was ransacked. Everything was in its place. He went to Lisa's bedroom first and knocked on the door. When no one answered he tried the knob but it was locked. *She keeps her room locked? I guess I would, too, if I had someone who just got out of prison stay with me.* He checked the bathroom next, and then he finally opened up the door to his room. The room was trashed. He quickly looked through all the drawers, the closet and then the boxes that were now totally empty. The papers were thrown all over the place. He wondered if he should call the police, but then decided not to bother. He dealt with them once today already. If the detective calls him back, he will let him know. As he was putting the papers back in order Lisa walked into the room.

"The door was wide open!" she exclaimed.

"Yes, it was open when I came in so I didn't close it in case I had to make a quick getaway. I checked your room and the door was locked. It looks like someone came in and trashed mine!" Lisa quickly walked out of his room and went to check hers. After a few moments, she reappeared.

"No one touched my room. That's odd. Is anything missing? Did you call the police?" she asked Anthony, who was still putting things back where they belonged.

"No, I didn't call yet. I waited for you to come home. I don't think I have anything missing, either. I called that detective twice today and he didn't answer his phone. I even stopped by the station and he wasn't there, as well."

"Did something else happen today?" she nervously asked him.

"I went to pick up my birth certificate today and when I stepped out to the car the driver side window was smashed and there was a note on the seat that read "I WARNED YOU!" so I called the detective and then the police cause he didn't answer. After work, I stopped at the mechanics to pick up the fixed car, and then I went to the police station to see him. I ran into Officer Tucker, though, and he sent his regards to you."

"This is so weird, stop cleaning up!" she ordered. "I am going to call the police, we need to file a report." She stepped out of the room and made the call. About twenty minutes later, a few officers arrived. Anthony, once again today, gave them the details as they wrote out the report. Meanwhile, Lisa was showing the room to a couple of other officers who opened up their kits and started to dust everything. They checked the whole apartment for fingerprints. Four hours later, the police had left the apartment, and Lisa called the building manager to have the locks changed. She wasn't taking any chances.

"I called the building manager. He said he will have someone swing by right away. Do you still want to get dinner? Jo said she will join us," she said to Anthony, as she joined him in his room.

"Honestly, not really. I just want to stay in tonight. It's been a hell of a day." *Although it would be great to see Jo again.* "I ran into Jo earlier today while I was waiting for my birth certificate."

"You did?" she asked, surprised. "I talked to her and she didn't mention it."

"Does she tell you everything?" Anthony asked as he continued to clean up the mess.

"For the most part," Lisa said. *At least I thought she did.* Lisa started to help him pick up the papers that were all over the bed and the floor. "There, all done." She smiled as they put away the last of the papers. "I'll go out and grab us some Chinese food. I should be back in about twenty minutes."

"Okay, I'll take a shower in the meantime," Anthony replied, and watched Lisa walk out of his room.

He took his shower and then shaved, thinking that he might as well do it now as opposed to the morning . He put on a black sweatshirt and a pair of flannel pajama pants and went to the living room where Lisa was waiting for him. The Chinese food was out on the table along with a bottle of red wine and a couple of glasses. She had changed clothes and now wore a black pair of yoga pants and a long-sleeved blue shirt.

"I either took a really long shower, or you are really fast," Anthony said to her as he sat down next to her on the couch. "Are you sure you want to do the wine thing? It was really hot in here after we drank that bottle the other day." Her watched her pale face turn pink and smiled.

"I'm fine with the wine. If it gets too hot in here I have a fire extinguisher we can use." They both laughed. and Anthony realized how much he really liked Lisa and how much he enjoyed her company.

A man came by and changed the locks on the door. He gave them each a copy of the new key, and left.

"Who else had the key to this place?" Anthony asked her.

"No one," she replied. *Except for Rob who never returned the key to her place when they broke up.* "That's why I think that it's weird. The door wasn't jammed. Whoever it was has a copy of the key. Which is why I'm glad that the locks are changed. If we didn't do that I wouldn't be able to sleep here, to tell you the truth. "

They spent the next couple of hours talking, wining and dining. Anthony, for the time being, had forgotten about the day's events and was able to relax a little.

"It's almost eleven," Anthony pointed out as he looked at his phone.

"Oh, my," Lisa replied as she started to gather things from the table. Anthony helped and in a matter of minutes, everything was clean. The leftovers were placed in the refrigerator and everything else, along with the empty bottle of wine, was disposed of. "I guess it's time to call it a night."

"Yes, I guess that it is. I had a really great time tonight, thank you," Anthony said as he smiled at her.

"Me, too," she smiled back and he went for it. He kissed her gently on her soft lips and after a couple of minutes, just when things were starting to heat up, he reluctantly pulled away.

"Good night," he simply said and walked away, while Lisa stood there completely speechless. The kiss blew her mind and she was left wanting more.

Chapter 13

The next day, Anthony woke up in a pool of sweat. He had another nightmare. The same man from the previous dream was chasing him down an alley. He flung himself at Anthony and knocked him down onto the cold, hard pavement. The man turned him around and as he was about to stab him with a knife, Anthony woke up. Feeling anxious, as if expecting something else to happen today, he somehow managed to get up. He joined Lisa in the kitchen, who made the coffee and a few pieces of toast.

"Good morning. Sleep well?" she asked him as he approached her. "You don't look so well today." He was pale skinned, but today he was ashen white.

"I feel okay," he replied as he poured himself a cup of coffee. "I just didn't sleep well last night. Too much on my mind, I guess. How about you?"

"I was up most of the time tossing and turning. Having known that someone else was here makes me feel a little violated." She thought that it was Rob who broke in. He is the only other person with a key. She called him last night to ask him and he denied that it was him. And then he advised her to go stay somewhere else or to kick Anthony out before something else happens.

"I'm sorry," he said with the utmost sincerity. "This is all my fault. I'll look around today for a place. It's been a couple of weeks, and I should be getting some money back as well. Howard said there is a place in North Olmsted that has a couple of apartments for rent. I'll give them each a call today. Hopefully there is a place that's still available."

"No, Anthony. Please don't," she pleaded. "I feel more safe with you here right now than if I was left by myself. At least until they find out who is causing all of this trouble."

"The things that have been happening have been horrible. I really don't want you or anyone to get hurt."

"I know, just please wait a little longer," she said as she took the last sip of her coffee. *I really like having you around.* "I need to go. I'll talk to you later?" she asked hopefully.

"Yes. I'll talk to you later. Why don't we have dinner out tonight?"

"Okay. I'll ask Jo as well." *I want to see what's going on with her.* "Bye," she called out as she closed the apartment door.

Anthony left soon after and as he was driving into work, he finally received a phone call from Detective Frank.

"Sorry I didn't get back to you yesterday. I had some problems at home I needed to take care of. What happened?" Detective Frank asked him.

Anthony told him about all of the events that occurred the previous day. When Anthony finished talking, the detective told him that he would take a look at the reports that were filed and will see if any new fingerprints showed up at either scene. He told him that if anything turned up he would let him know. Anthony parked his car in a little lot next to the building where he worked.

He walked into the building all the while checking his back. He didn't know why exactly he was all that freaked out. The two nightmares that he had were so vivid and seemed so real. He hoped that they don't become a reality. The prison where he had stayed was a lot more dangerous. He learned very quickly early on to just stay in his locked cell when he was given the opportunity and he always kept himself locked in. He was lucky enough to have a cell of his own. He had made just one friend while he was there, and he stayed away from everyone else. The things those men did to each other in there are horrible. He made it safely to his office where he automatically went to work drawing up plans for the new hotel. The deadline for the plans was just a few weeks away. He was feeling uneasy so he didn't leave his office at all. At five, Anthony left to go home.

He entered the lobby of the apartment building, and noticed Rob Tucker walking out of the elevator. There were so many people walking around in the lobby that Anthony didn't think that Rob saw him on his way out. Anthony picked up the mail and he quickly ran up the stairs to check the apartment. He knew Lisa was home because he had parked his car next to hers in the garage. She was sitting on the couch when he came into the apartment. She jumped at the loud bang the door made when it swung open.

"You okay?" he asked her, out of breath from running up those stairs.

"Yes, what's the matter?"

"Nothing. I saw that Officer Tucker, leaving. I thought that maybe something happened to you. Why was he here?"

"He heard what happened last night and dropped by to check on me, that's all." She smiled. "There's nothing to worry about. Can you please close the door? It's getting cold in here." She quickly changed the subject. She didn't feel like explaining Rob to him right now. He closed the door and put his coat on the rack and joined her in the living room.

"You're home early?" he asked.

"Yes. I took an early day today. I finished up what I had to do and came straight home. I don't need to go to court until next week. I talked with Jo and she said that she and Bob will join us tonight, so just let me know what you feel like having for dinner, and what time I should let Jo know to meet us."

Afraid of something else happening today, he suggested, "How about we order some pizza and have the two of them come over. Maybe we can play some cards. I became an expert while in prison, playing with my only friend." His name was Jack and he never told Anthony what he was in for, and Anthony never pried. He was glad that he had some company, and because of Jack, all of the other inmates left Anthony alone.

"Okay, sounds fine with me. You know how to play rummy? That's my favorite card game."

"I sure do," he answered. "I'm going to go change, and you can make the phone calls."

He went in to his room and looked around. Everything seemed as if it was untouched since last night. He took off his suit jacket and when he laid it on the bed a piece of paper fell out of the inside pocket. *My birth certificate. I forgot all about it.* He left it alone until he changed out of his work clothes. He put the clothes on the hangers and into the closet. He sat on the edge of his bed and opened the birth certificate. Anthony Rozman, born at Fairview

Hospital on March 7, 1976. Mother: Mary Travino, and father: Jerry Brickman. *What the hell?* All of these years and he just found out now that his real father is someone else. *Is this why my mom keeps calling me Jerry? Do I look like my father?? I can't believe this! I can't believe that the both of them didn't tell me! Does Lisa know?* He quickly left the room and went to the kitchen where Lisa was standing and on the phone. As soon as she put the phone down he handed her the certificate.

"I just found out that my father wasn't my birth father!" he exclaimed. "Did you know this?" She sighed and breathed out, "Yes, I did know. I'm sorry."

"Why in the hell didn't you tell me?"

"I didn't think that it was my place to say anything. That's a family matter."

"Did your detective that helped you with my case find him? Is he alive?" He had so many questions for her. Before she could answer, the doorbell rang.

"I should get that, it's probably Jo and Bob. We'll talk later," she told him as she went to open the door. She was right it was Jo and Bob. They walked in and had a seat in the living room. Anthony decided to join them.

"How is it going?" he asked them as he took a seat on the other couch.

"Not bad," Bob replied first. "How about you? Anything new?"

"Not really, just work," Anthony replied.

"The pizza should be here shortly. What would you guys like to drink?" Lisa asked.

"I will take some water," Bob responded.

Jo thought about it for a minute and said she will have the same.

"I will get my own," Anthony said, as he followed Lisa to the kitchen. Lisa took out a couple of bottles of water out of the fridge, while Anthony grabbed a can of Pepsi and popped it open. They joined Bob and Jo and talked with them until the pizza arrived. They played a couple of rounds of rummy and ate the pizza when Bob finally yawned and hinted to Jo that it was time to leave. Jo ignored the hint and shuffled the cards.

"It's time to go," Bob said, "it's getting late." All three of them checked the time and it was almost eleven.

"Yes, it is late," Jo said as she put the cards on the table. "Thank you for a good time," she said to Lisa and Anthony. She stood up and walked to the door where she grabbed their coats off of the rack. Bob, Lisa and Anthony all followed her. They said their goodbyes and Lisa locked the door after they walked out.

"That was fun!" she exclaimed to Anthony as she went to clear up the mess that was left behind.

"Yes, it was fun. I need some questions answered Lisa, so tell me everything that you know that I don't. Please."

"Let me clean this mess up first and then we'll sit and talk." She took her time, all the while thinking about exactly what and how much she will say. She didn't want to break her promise to Jerry, even though he is dead. When she was finished with the clean-up, she joined Anthony in the living room who was staring at his birth certificate with a pained look. She sat down next to him and started to talk. "What exactly do you want to know?"

"For starters, I want to know how come you didn't mention this to me?"

"I thought that you knew," she nervously replied. He shook his head and rolled his eyes.

"Did you have the private investigator look into this?"

"Yes, I did. He told me that Jerry Brickman died in 2007."

"Do I have any brothers or sisters? Is his wife still alive?"

"You had one brother who is dead, and one half-sister who lives in California. We didn't look her up because we didn't think that it was pertinent to the case. The wife died a couple of years ago."

"This is unbelievable!" he exclaimed. "I wonder why my mom and dad didn't tell me this. I can't believe that they kept this secret from me," he said as he put his head down in his palms and rubbed his forehead with his long fingers.

"I'm sorry." She lightly caressed his knee with her hand and felt a surge of electricity move from her hand throughout her whole body.

He moved his hands from his face and put them at his side. He looked at her with eyes full of tears and asked, "Is there anything else about me that you know that I don't?"

"No," she replied. Anthony grabbed her chin and moved her head so that his eyes were directly looking at hers.

"Really?" he asked again.

"Yes," she replied, and as she closed her eyes, he kissed her. But not softly and patiently like before. This time, it was powerful and more urgent. This time, he didn't quit. With a strong force, he pulled her legs up on the couch beside him, then lay on top of her, never letting his mouth off of hers. As their tongues meshed, his hand squeezed and rubbed the outer side of her thigh and she started

to moan as his groin rubbed her. He didn't stop and she didn't want

him to.

Chapter 14

The next morning, she woke up in his bed, lying next to him. He had his arm and leg wrapped around her and she couldn't move. She had no idea what came over her last night. The sensations she felt had overpowered her and she couldn't resist. It was the most amazing experience she ever had. Without wanting to wake him, up she carefully slid off the bed. She grabbed a sweatshirt that was on the floor of his room and put it on. She turned around to see whether he was awake and smiled when she saw that he was sleeping. She went to wash up. As she looked at herself in the mirror she thought *I can't believe it. I can't believe that we had sex. Not once but twice.* She splashed her face with the warm water and then patted it dry with a towel. Lisa felt guiltier this morning than she had before. Not because she had sex, but because of the lies and the secret she was keeping. She realized this morning, when she woke up she not only liked Anthony, but loved him. Although she thought the same thing yesterday about Rob. He kissed her yesterday on his way out and as much as she didn't want to admit it, she still had feelings for him. She quickly went to her room to change. Her mind was in overdrive as she tried to sort all of her feelings. How does Anthony feel about her? Did he have sex with her because he hadn't had it in a long time? Was it because she was willing and available?

Anthony was in the kitchen pouring coffee when Lisa walked in. She was wearing a pair of brown slacks and a black v-neck sweater.

"How ya doing?" he casually asked her as she sat down on the stool by the counter.

"I am okay," she replied and managed to smile. She didn't want him to notice her discomfort. He looked so handsome in his dark gray sweats and white t-shirt. "Sleep well?"

"Fantastic!" he countered and smiled. He had a great night and all he thought about right now was grabbing her again and taking her back to the bedroom. He knew he was horny but he also knew that he could control himself. Last night was different. It was magical and he just couldn't stop himself. He grabbed a cup of coffee and handed it to her. "I hope that I didn't do anything wrong last night. I didn't hurt you, did I?"

"No," she answered, as she sipped her coffee. "I need to get going, though. Are we doing anything tonight?"

"I don't know how late I'll be," he replied. "I'm planning on visiting mom tonight after work." He was hoping his mom could give him some answers.

"Okay, then I will see you later." She got up off the stool and started to walk away when he grabbed her elbow and turned her around to face him.

"I hope you have a good day." He smiled, and then kissed her. Surprised by his action, she stared at him for a second, and then said, "I hope you have a good day as well."

Anthony was a little late to work this morning and to his amazement neither Nick nor Howard was in the office. The secretary, Julia, was there and she nodded at him when he entered. He walked straight into his office and sat down on his swivel chair. He felt so many different emotions racing through his mind. So much was happening and he didn't know what to sort out first, or how to even begin. He had no idea who framed him, he was shocked to learn that his dad wasn't his father, and now he had to figure out his feelings for Lisa as well.

At about 10 a.m., Nick walked into Anthony's office and awoke him from his daydreaming.

"Did you get anything done for the hotel project?" Nick asked him. "We have a meeting on Friday of next week with the new owner. I want to show him a couple of ideas."

"I have one that is almost done, and one that I just started to work on. I can be done with the both of them before Friday. Have you talked with Howard? I tried calling him this morning and he didn't answer his phone."

"I haven't talked to him this morning," Nick replied. "Which is odd. He usually calls me in the morning to let me know if he won't be coming in."

"I'll keep calling. If I don't get in touch with him, I'll take a ride to his house."

"Okay, that's good," Nick said, as he started to walk out. "Let me know if you get ahold of him."

Toward noon and still not being able to get ahold of Howard, Anthony was starting to worry. He decided to give Lisa a call to let her know that he would most likely swing by Howard's after work. She told him to try not to worry, and that Howard was just probably not feeling well. But that didn't help to ease his mind when he had such a horrible feeling about it. After he hung up with Lisa he decided to call Detective Frank. He wanted to know if there was any progress in the case. Even that phone call didn't do him any good. The detective had told him that he didn't get any new leads. He went back to work and thought that he would finish the plans for the first design before leaving today. This way he would at least have one thing that he wouldn't have to worry about.

He clicked "save" on the computer and decided to save the design on his flash drive as well. *With my luck these days, I need to have a backup,* he thought, as he pulled the flash drive out of his laptop and shut off the computer. As he put the laptop in its case, he heard a knock on the door and looked up to see Jo standing in the doorway. She wore a navy blue dress shirt and a pair of black slacks. Her brown hair was curly and fell on top of her slender shoulders. He was surprised to see her and smiled.

"Hi," he said as she started to walk in. "This is a nice surprise."

"I was in the building and thought I would say hello," she smiled.

"Are you working on a story?" He knew she was a reporter and worked for *The Plain Dealer.*

"Yes, there are a few local artists that rent a space on the upper floor. I stopped by to interview a couple of them. Are you almost done? I was thinking that maybe we could get a cup of coffee."

He looked at his watch. It was 4:30.

"I would actually like that very much," Anthony said. "Just give me a minute to gather my things." He was really looking forward to this.

Jo drove and took him to a quiet café in the Tremont area. The place was small and only a couple of other people were in there. He ordered a cappuccino and she grabbed some kind of herbal tea. They spent a few seconds arguing over who was going to pay and Anthony was the first to concede. They walked over to a small table in the corner of the Civilization Café, and sat down.

"Do you come here often?" Anthony asked her and took his first sip of the cappuccino. As the hot, steamy coffee went down his throat, he thought it burned everything on the inside. He opened his eyes and exclaimed, "Holy, shit! This has got to be the hottest coffee I have ever had!" Jo started to laugh hysterically at his expression, and Anthony joined in. Jo had a cute, contagious laugh. Anthony just couldn't help himself.

After chitchatting for about twenty minutes, Anthony decided that it was time to go. As much as he enjoyed the company, he needed to go see Howard. He still hadn't heard from him. Jo drove him back to the office parking lot where he had left his car.

"Would you like for me to go with you?" she kindly asked him, as he put his hand on the door handle.

"No, thanks. I think I should go alone. I plan on picking up some chicken soup and hanging out with Howard tonight," Anthony replied. "Thanks again for the coffee. I had a really great time. Maybe we can do it again."

"I would like that," she smiled, and Anthony went to his car and drove off.

He stopped at Marie's Restaurant and grabbed two chicken noodle soups to go and then headed straight to Howard's house. He parked his car in the driveway right behind Howard's midnight blue Ford Escape. He knocked on the door. After a couple of minutes of standing out in the cold, Anthony knocked a little louder. He went around to the back of the house and walked up the two steps that led to a wooden deck and the back door to the house. The patio had a nice roof. The roof was wooden and it covered the whole back deck. It was held up by four wooden posts and there were triangular shapes at the corners. Anthony remembered designing it for Howard. It was his first job. He walked up to the screen door and opened it. Once again he knocked and this time yelled out,

"Howard, it's Anthony let me in." He couldn't wait any longer. Nervously, he looked to the side of the porch and remembered that Howard used to have an extra key on top of the two by four that formed the bottom of the triangle. He quickly walked over to it, and on tiptoes, felt the top of the piece of wood. *Aha, got it!* He grabbed it, and then quickly walked to the door. He unlocked it, entered, and closed the door behind him.

"Howard!" he yelled out as he searched the kitchen and then walked to the living room. There, he saw Howard lying face down on the floor by the smashed up coffee table. Anthony ran over to him. "Howard, Howard!" He turned him over and saw the knife sticking out of his stomach and the blood that was oozing out. He checked Howard's pulse and felt the vein slowly throbbing against his shaking fingers. He took out his phone and called 911. After what seemed like an eternity, the EMS arrived, as well as the police. Detective Frank showed up, too. He questioned Anthony. When Anthony felt that he had enough of the implication that he was the one who had done it, he looked at the detective and angrily said, "I need to go to the hospital now. If you have any other questions, call me."

He ran out of the house and into the Hummer. He was lucky enough to have been informed that Howard would be taken to MetroHealth Hospital. He drove like a maniac and made it to the hospital in minutes. He walked through the emergency room doors and waited in a line to talk with someone. When his turn came, he inquired about Howard. He lied and told the receptionist that he was his son. He knew that she wouldn't have given him any information otherwise. She told him that the patient is in surgery and gave him directions where to go. He quickly walked through the sliding doors and went to the waiting area. Once there, he grabbed a seat, and decided to call Lisa.

"Hey," he said when she answered and then, without a pause, he went on to tell her everything that happened. When he finished telling her that Detective Frank had grilled him and had implied that he was the one who did it, she finally spoke up,

"You need to calm down, Anthony." She could swear that she felt his pounding heart through the telephone. She could feel his frustration and negative energy flowing through to her. "Any news on Howard? Did anyone come out to talk to you yet?"

"No. I'm waiting. All I know is that he is in surgery."

"Okay. I am leaving the office right now and will be there in like fifteen minutes."

"Okay," he started to say as he eyed Detective Frank walking toward him. "The detective is here," he mumbled.

"I'm coming," she said and hung up.

The detective stood in front of him and asked, "Any news?"

"No, not yet," Anthony replied as Detective Frank sat in a chair next to him. "You know, Howard is like a father to me. I would never hurt him." The detective nodded and didn't say a word. They both sat and waited. The sliding doors opened and a doctor came out with a nurse. He walked over to the receptionist and asked her something. She pointed to Anthony and the doctor walked over to them.

"Hi," he said as Anthony stood up, "My name is Dr. Schaab. You are Mr. Filiere's son?"

"Yes, I am," Anthony replied and surprisingly the detective didn't dispute his answer. "Is he okay?"

"He was stabbed on his left side of his abdomen and his kidney was punctured. He will be okay. We were able to remove the kidney with no problems. He had lost a lot of blood and we had to give him a blood transfusion. He is in ICU and you can visit with him now. If you have any other questions, please just give me a call." He handed his card to Anthony, and gave one to the detective as well. They shook hands and the doctor walked away.

"I'm glad that he will be okay," the detective said to Anthony.

"Yes, me too." Anthony breathed a sigh of relief.

"I'll be in touch," Detective Frank said and walked away. He was greeted by Lisa.

"Detective," she nodded as he stopped. "What happened? Any news?" she asked him.

"Mr. Filiere is out of surgery and it looks like he will be fine. They just moved him to ICU."

"Someone is really out to get Anthony again," she said.

"It appears that way," he replied. "I need to go, I'll keep in touch. Make sure that he doesn't leave town. He isn't out of the woods just yet."

"I'll make sure of that, detective," she said, as he put his hand on her shoulder.

"And be careful, this isn't a game. People are getting hurt."

She nodded and walked down the hall to catch up with Anthony. As soon as she saw him she hugged him. She felt horrible about Howard and wanted to comfort him.

"I got here as soon as I could. I saw the detective on his way out. Did you get the room number yet?" she asked as she pulled away.

"Yes, I did. I'm going to go there right now. I want to be there when he wakes up."

"I'll go with you. He grabbed her hand and led her through the doors and down the cold hall.

*   *

He has been watching her for the last two weeks, and he couldn't believe what he had just witnessed. He saw her at the hospital with Anthony. He couldn't believe that she had a thing for him. The way that she looked at him, her eyes showing concern, and the affection that she had shown Anthony said it all. Not long ago, Lisa looked at him that way. He thought that she loved him. And yet the love that he had for her wasn't enough to stop him from the vengeful path he chose. Before he left, he made her promise not to tell a soul, and he was certain that she did. He was disappointed and now was certain that he was going to do more damage. He was angry at her. He was angry that she had helped Anthony get out of prison, and now he was even angrier after witnessing the love that she had shown Anthony.

Disguised as a vagrant, he carefully left the hospital and went back to his retreat. *No one will be able to figure it out,* he thought as he made it to his house. He went to the bathroom to take off the nasty old clothes that he was wearing, and took a shower to wash off the garbage stench. When he dressed in normal clothes, he walked out and went to the kitchen to grab a beer from the fridge. He lit up a cigarette and deeply inhaled the nicotine, and then slowly breathed out the smoke. *Much better. Now I can relax and carefully plan out my next move.* The scenarios he created in his mind gave him a headache and he chain-smoked throughout the evening, drinking all of the beer he had. Anger rose up his throat and caused a foul taste in his mouth. *She will pay for this!*

In the ICU, Anthony and Lisa sat by Howard and waited for Howard to wake up from the anesthesia. Every few minutes a nurse would walk in, check all the monitors, and leave. They each sat in a chair close to each other, and not once did Anthony let go of her hand. They sat in silence, and he felt so much better with her by his side. He sat and watched Howard. He would have been devastated if he didn't make it. He finally took his eyes off him and looked at Lisa. She managed to give him a comforting, small smile.

"Howard has always been by my side. He was always there to help me and now I am going to do everything I can to be there for him. I don't know who's doing this. I wish I did," he whispered to her.

"Me, too. I hope the detective figures it out. The sooner the better." She had no idea what was going on and was sick of it all. She was just as puzzled as he was. This whole time she thought that Rob was just trying to scare them so that Anthony would no longer stay with her. *There is no way that Rob would hurt someone. Would he?* She shivered at the thought and felt every hair on her body stand up.

"You cold, huh?" he asked her as he let go of her hand and put his arm around her. He moved closer to her and her head rested on his shoulder.

Chapter 15

She stepped out of the room to take a walk and get some coffee. Howard still hadn't awakened. She needed to stretch her legs and offered to go get some coffee for the two of them. Her phone rang and Jo was on the caller ID, so she answered,

"Hello."

"Hey," she replied, "how are you?"

"Pretty crappy," Lisa replied. "I'm at MetroHealth. Howard Filiere was stabbed. Anthony found him at his house and called 911."

"Oh my God," Jo exclaimed. "How horrible! Is he going to be okay?"

"Yes, he will be, thank God! I feel just horrible for Anthony. He is pretty shaken up about it."

"I can imagine. Is there anything I can do?"

"No, that's okay. I am walking now to the cafeteria. I think I'll grab him something to eat as well. It's almost eight. Hopefully, we won't stay here too much longer."

"Okay, I'll let you go. Let me know if you need anything."

"Thanks Jo. I'll call you tomorrow." She hung up. As she neared the cafeteria, her phoned beeped. She looked at it and it was a text message from Rob that read "Need to talk ASAP." She didn't reply. She ordered two large coffees and a couple of blueberry muffins. The sandwiches that they offered didn't look appealing. On her way back to the room she spotted Rob waiting by the door of the ICU room.

"Lisa, we need to talk. Didn't you get my message?" He was angry.

"I got it. I can't leave now!" she whispered. She didn't want Anthony to hear them.

"You need to meet me tomorrow morning. I'll be waiting at your office at 8 a.m. If anything happens, you need to call me right away. You understand?!" he squeezed her elbow and she almost spilled the coffee.

"Okay. I'll be there, Rob. What the hell is your problem?"

"My problem is that he is staying with you, and people are getting hurt. Don't you see you could be a target? You need to stay the hell away from him!" he scolded her, and it was loud enough for Anthony to hear voices coming from outside the room.

Anthony opened the door and walked out to see Rob and Lisa standing in the hall.

"What's going on?" he interrupted the two of them. Rob removed his hand from Lisa's elbow, and turned to face him.

"You!" Rob exclaimed, "you need to put an end to this. I don't know why you are hurting everyone around you, but you need to stop!"

"I'm not doing anything!" Anthony retorted. "I want this all to end as much as you do. I'm not hurting anyone! I didn't murder those women then, and I sure as hell didn't hurt Howard now."

"I am watching you like a hawk," Rob said and turned toward Lisa. "And you need to watch it. I have a feeling that you are next on the list. I need to go, I'll see you in the morning. Frank will have an officer here to watch Mr. Filiere, but you two are on your own." He walked away from them and left the hospital.

Rob Tucker was just as confused as everyone else. He was driving home and the whole time his thoughts were on Anthony and Lisa. He had been in communication with Detective Frank and there is no proof Anthony was behind any of this. Originally, they both thought that Anthony was sending these threats to himself. They thought for sure he was doing it, so that he wouldn't go back to prison. After talking with Frank earlier today, they were both leaning towards Anthony being innocent. *I know who murdered the three women, but it would be impossible for him to come back. Who could be doing all of this? Lisa? She has nothing to gain. I know what her secret is. Is she that desperate to actually hurt someone, rather then not let Anthony find out? I can't wait to grill her in the morning.*

A couple of hours later, Howard woke up. He was confused and had no idea where he was or what had happened that day. He did, however, remember who he was and who Anthony was. The police officer who was securing the door called Detective Frank and told him the news. Not long after, Frank came back to MetroHealth. He walked in the room and introduced himself to Howard. He told Anthony and Lisa to leave the room, and once the door was closed, and with no small talk, the detective started with the questions.

"Mr. Filiere, do you know why you are here?"

"The doctor told me that I was stabbed, had a kidney removed, but I will recover."

"Can you tell me what you did today? Start from when you woke up, please. I know that you are tired, but the sooner I get the information, the sooner I can find whoever is responsible."

"To tell you the truth, detective, I really don't remember anything at all. I don't even remember waking up today."

"What's the last thing that you do remember?"

"I remember going to bed last night."

"Do you remember when?"

"I remember that it was later than normal. It was around 11:30."

"Did you drink any alcohol or take any medicine last night?"

"I had a glass of red wine at dinner. But that's all. I didn't take any medicine. Why do you ask?"

"Just standard procedure, Mr. Filiere. Do you remember where you had dinner last night?"

"I had dinner with an old school friend of mine, at a little place in downtown Willoughby," he answered.

"Can you tell me the name of the restaurant and the friend you went there with?" Tiring and with a laboring breath, Howard struggled to answer Detective Frank. So instead, he reached for the detective's notebook and pen. He managed to scribble the information down, and handed the notebook back to the detective. "Thank you, if you remember anything at all about today's events, could you please give me a call right away?" He handed Howard his card.

"I sure will, detective," Howard replied. "Do you think that this is all related somehow to Anthony?"

"Right now, we do. There is an officer here to watch over you just in case the culprit reappears. Be very careful, Mr. Filiere. We'll be in touch." The detective shook Howard's hand and stepped out of the room. Anthony, Lisa and an officer were standing in the hallway, conversing. "You guys can go back in now," he said to them. "I need to leave. Let me know right away if Mr. Filiere remembers anything." He turned to the officer, nodded, then left.

Anthony and Lisa walked back in to the room and waited there with Howard until he was placed in a regular room. After 1 a.m., Howard was settled in room 315. They said their goodnights, and driving separately, left the hospital. Anthony had wanted to ask Lisa a few questions of his own, but not having the time or privacy to talk with Lisa about the visit she had with Rob, he decided to wait until they got home.

"Lisa, what did Tucker want with you today?" he asked her as she took her coat off and placed it on the rack.

"He was concerned and stopped by to make sure that I was okay, that's all," Lisa responded.

"Are you two together? I was under the assumption that you weren't dating anyone. Now I feel horrible!"

She walked over to where he was standing and put her arms around his waist.

"You don't have anything to worry about when it comes to me." She smiled and kissed him. "You had a real horrible day today. You should go to bed. I plan on taking a nice long bath and hitting the bed myself. I need to get up early."

"You going to join me afterwards?" Anthony asked as he took his hands off her hips.

She thought about it for a moment, and replied.

"Maybe, I will check in on you when I get out of the bathroom. So why don't you go to bed." He nodded and left the livingroom. Lisa took her cellphone out and looked to see why it was vibrating. Two messages; one from Rob, and one from Jo. She looked at Jo's first.

"How is everything? Are you home yet? Do you need anything? Call me."

Lisa replied, "Fine, at home, and will call you in the morning. Night."

She heard Anthony as the door to his room closed. She walked to her room to grab her things. *Should I sleep with Anthony tonight?* she thought as she was rummaging through her drawers. *Aha. This will work.* She pulled out a gray PJ dress that had three-quarter length sleeves and it came up to just above her knees. *It's simple and cute.* She went into the bathroom and turned on the bathtub faucet. She looked at her phone and read the message from Rob, "See you in the morning." She replied an "OK" and put the phone on the sink as she got ready to get into the tub. She thought about Rob and Anthony as she settled into the water. She still thought that she had feelings for Rob. He looked so good today dressed in a black suit. For a minute, she wished that he never dumped her. Anthony, on the other hand, was sweet, and seemed so caring. He was genuine, and he made her heart pulsate. She wondered if the sensations that she felt when with him, he felt as well.

While Lisa was enjoying her bath, Anthony decided to sneak into her room. He wanted to see if she had anything to hide. He crept out of his room and stopped in front of the bathroom door. He heard the water splashing and continued. He slowly turned the knob to her room and the door opened. While straining to hear Lisa in the bathroom, he turned on the lights and scanned the room. To his surprise, the room was pretty plain. There was a king sized

bed that had a brown comforter that complimented the off-white color of the walls. There was a dresser, empty on top, with a mirror. The two nightstands on either side of the bed had lamps on them. One of them had a book on it along with her glasses. As he heard the toilet flush he turned off the lights and quickly went back to his bedroom. He was expecting to at least see pictures spread all over. The only picture that was in the room, hung above the bed, was a replica of Monet's *Water Lilies*.

Chapter 16

The next morning, Lisa woke up, in Anthony's arms, to the sound of the alarm. She smiled as she turned off the alarm and carefully got out of bed. She closed the bedroom and went to the kitchen to make a pot of coffee. She then proceeded to the bathroom where she brushed her teeth and washed her face. Once done, she opened the door and almost ran into Anthony who was standing by it. He grabbed her hips and pulled her to him.

"Morning," he said and kissed her. She responded and put her hands behind his neck and ran her fingers through his soft hair. The little kiss had now turned into much more as he pushed her against the wall and slid his hands up the back of her thighs, at the same time lifting her PJs along with them. He moved his lips off hers just long enough to remove the PJs and throw them on the floor. He lifted her up and carried her back to his room where he dropped her on his bed and lay on top of her.

*   *

Rob had been waiting for Lisa outside of her office for the last twenty minutes. *Where the hell is she?* He leaned against the door and called her. She didn't pick up and he didn't leave a message. He texted her and decided to wait a few more minutes before he ends up going to her apartment. A few minutes later, his phone rang and he answered,

"Where have you been?! I've been waiting here for the last 30 minutes."

"I'm almost there. Sorry, I like totally overslept," Lisa answered as she felt her face heat up and blush when she thought about what she had been doing for the last 30 minutes. *Thank God, Rob can't see me through the phone.* "I'll be there in a few minutes."

"Okay," Rob replied and hung up the phone.

A few minutes later, Lisa appeared and unlocked the door to the office. Rob walked in behind her and shut the door. She casually walked around to her desk and put her briefcase and coat on her chair. She wasn't going to let Rob know how much he intimidated her. She folded her arms and put on her best poker face.

"What's so important that you need to talk to me?" she asked as he sat on the chair opposite to where she was standing.

"Are you doing all of this, Lisa?" he asked her.

"Doing what?"

"Are you the one that's sending all the letters and threats? More importantly, are you the one who hurt Mr. Filiere yesterday?"

Lisa started to laugh at the accusation.

"That's pretty funny, Rob. I was going to ask you the same thing."

He looked at her with a puzzled face.

"Why would I do that?!"

"I don't know, to scare me? You're the one that didn't want him to stay with me!" *Maybe he still loves me?* "And besides, why would I?" she yelled back. "Look, if I didn't do it, and if you didn't do it someone else is out there."

"Now you're getting somewhere, Lisa," Rob sarcastically said, as he stood up and crossed his arms. "Someone is out there, and you need to let me know what's going on. If anything unusual happens, call me right away. Do you understand?" She nodded and he walked over to her. He moved her chin up with his hand and looked directly in her eyes, "I would never hurt you. You need to believe me when I tell you this." Her face was as pale, and for a second she thought that she was going to be sick. He leaned over her and lightly kissed her on the lips. He stepped back a little. "I know that you and Anthony have something going on, but I am here for you. I mean it. Please call me if you need me." She was frozen and barely managed to nod as she watched him walk out of the office.

Anthony was late to work, as well, and as he walked into the building he ran into Jim. Jim was a mutual friend of Howard's and Nick's who had an office on the floor above theirs.

"Morning," Jim said as he extended his hand to shake his. "Welcome back."

"Thanks Jim. It's good to see you."

"I just talked with Nick, he said he heard from Howard earlier this morning. I'm glad that he made it," Jim said with the utmost sincerity.

"Me, too." Anthony replied. "I feel horrible and feel like it's all my fault."

"Don't think like that, Anthony. It is not your fault. Some lunatic is out there, and I hope the police find him before he hurts someone else." Anthony sighed. "Thanks, Jim. I need to get going. Hopefully we will get together for lunch soon." Anthony shook his hand again and walked away. He first went in to talk with Nick. He wanted to give him all of the designs he had for the project he had been working on, and most importantly he wanted to let Nick know that he won't be back until the police find the culprit. He packed up all of his belongings and left the building. From there, he went to the nursing home to see his mother.

He hated that nasty odor that you smell right when you walk into the home. He signed in with the receptionist and went to his mother's room. She was sitting in a chair by the window and was watching the snow melt from the trees.

"Hi, Mom!" he said loudly as he grabbed a chair and sat down next to her.

"Anthony, darling. How are you?" She smiled at him and she put her frail hand on top of his.

"You know who I am?"

"Yes, dear. Of course I do," she replied.

"Mom, can you tell me anything about my father?"

"Your dad was the kindest man I had ever known," she smiled. "The things he did for me I will always be grateful for."

"Mom, I want you to tell me something about my real father. Can you tell me about him? His name is Jerry. Do you remember him?"

Her smile faded and she was quiet for a moment.

"Come on, Mom," Anthony pleaded. "Please tell me who Jerry is."

"I wanted to be the one to tell you this." She spoke softly. "Jerry was a boy who I was in love with when I was in high school. He was everything to me. When I became pregnant, Jerry told me that we were going to get married. He said he loved me. But then out of nowhere, he stopped showing up to school, he stopped meeting up with me, and a few months later, he was married to another girl. Your dad, he was one of my closest friends. He married me so that I didn't get ridiculed by others. He took care of the both of us. For that I will always be grateful to him."

"You have never spoken to Jerry after that?" Anthony asked.

"Once, I saw him once, a few years later. We had talked and he explained himself to me. We wished each other well, and that was it."

"What did he say?"

"What difference does it make? We just weren't meant to be." she replied and looked back out the window. Anthony sighed and just held on to her hand. A few minutes later, she turned to him and asked, "Who are you? What do you want?" Without a reply, he stood up. Once again she asked, "Who are you?"

"It's Anthony, I need to go." He gave her a quick kiss on her forehead and left.

From the nursing home, he drove straight to the hospital to visit Howard. He felt horrible about Howard getting hurt and almost killed. Somehow it was all of his fault. He should have just stayed in prison, he thought as he drove onto the freeway. He is going to have to move out of Lisa's place. *It's best that I stay away from everyone until this all gets sorted out. The last thing I need is for Lisa to get hurt or even worse, get killed.* He dug through his wallet and found the number that he was looking for. He quickly called the number of the place in North Olmsted that was for rent. The manager told him that he would be able to move in immediately, and Anthony was happy about it. After discussing the terms with the building manager, Anthony accepted and said that he would stop by around noon with the deposit. He just hoped that Lisa wasn't going to be too upset about him moving out tonight.

He parked in the garage at the hospital, took the elevator to the third floor, and went to Howard's room. He was greeted by an officer at the door who checked his ID before letting him in to see Howard. He carefully opened the door, not wanting to make any noise in case Howard was asleep.

"Hi, Howard I'm surprised you're awake!" Anthony exclaimed as he took a seat on a chair next to him.

"I am wide awake," Howard replied. "It's too hard to sleep with the pain." Howard grimaced as he tried to sit up a little. Anthony adjusted the pillows and helped him get a little more comfortable.

"I am so sorry, Howard. I wish this never happened."

"I know. I just wish that I could remember what happened. The faster that I remember, the better for everyone. I noticed last night that you and Lisa were pretty friendly. You need to be careful, Anthony."

"You are absolutely right!" Anthony said. "Which is why I'll be moving out of her place tonight. I don't want anything to happen to her."

"Good. You found a place already?"

"Yup, I called the guy whose number you gave me. I am going to go there right when I leave here. I also told Nick that I won't be in until all of this is settled."

"Was he upset?" Howard asked.

"No, at least I don't think so. I gave him the designs that I have finished so at least he has something to go on. Do you want something to eat or drink? Do you want me to bring you anything later?"

"Actually, yes you can. I need some underwear, a robe, and maybe you can sneak me in a bottle of wine. I could really use a drink."

"Howard, you can't drink. But I promise when you get out, I'll take you somewhere nice for dinner and will let you drink away. I'll be back later with the underwear and some magazines."

"Okay. You should get going if you plan on moving out tonight," Howard said as he yawned.

"I will be back later. If you need anything else, then give me a call. I will be here around six." Anthony stood up and watched Howard close his eyes.

He left and went to the nearest bank to open up a checking account so that he could deposit the check that he received yesterday from the state. He was surprised at the amount. He was given $100,000 for each year that he was incarcerated and an extra $50,000 for being wrongfully convicted. The woman, Janie, was very nice and it didn't take long for him to get everything he needed done. He opened up two accounts; one checking and one savings. She gave him a few blank checks that he could use in the meantime, and $2,000 in cash. He gave her Lisa's address for now because he wanted to make sure that the real checks and deposit card are sent to the right place.

With time to spare before meeting with the building manager at noon, Anthony decided to go to the store to pick up everything that Howard needed. With plenty of shopping places in North Olmsted, he decided to go there. This way he can see the apartment on his way back downtown. After an hour of shopping, he was set and ready to meet up with the building manager. He left the store and made a right on Lorain Road. He drove just a few minutes and turned into a parking lot with the building address that he was given. He parked his car in front of a little building with a sign that read 'Building Manager'. He knocked on the door, and a little old, bald man opened it.

"You must be Mr. Rozman," he said, "please come in."

"Thank you for letting me stop by right away," Anthony said as he walked in.

"It's no problem," Mr. Huber said. "I owed Howard a favor. Now I can finally tell him to quit bugging me," Mr. Huber laughed out loud. "I owed him a favor since college. It took me 50 years to finally pay him back." He took a pair of keys out of the desk drawer. "Come on, let me show you the apartment first." He led Anthony across the parking lot. "This is the only one I have available. You have one bedroom, bathroom, kitchen, and living room. You also have your own laundry room with a washer and dryer." He unlocked the door and let Anthony in as he followed behind.

"This is great," Anthony said. The kitchen was updated and had all of the appliances. All he would have to get is a coffee maker and a microwave. He would need to get a living room set and a bedroom one, as well. The place had a fake wooden floor and he was thankful that it wasn't carpeted. "I can move in tonight?" He asked as he walked throughout the apartment.

"Yes, sir. I just need you to give me a deposit of $900.00 and sign the rental agreement."

Anthony walked back out into the cold and followed Mr. Huber back to his office. There, everything was finalized. The rent covered all of the utilities except for the cable and Anthony left Mr. Huber's office feeling great. It was almost 1:30 p.m., and he hadn't spoken to Lisa at all. He decided to pay her a visit at her office and surprise her with some coffee and doughnuts.

Lisa was all alone in her office and daydreaming when she heard a knock on the door. *Who could this be?* The door opened and Anthony walked in with a bag of Dunkin' Donuts and a couple of coffees.

"Hi," she said surprised to see him. She figured he was too busy with work since he hadn't texted her at all today. She didn't expect to see him, but was happy to.

"I brought you some doughnuts and a coffee." He smiled as he put the bag and coffee on her desk.

"Thank you," she smiled as she opened up the bag and took out a jelly doughnut. "This is my favorite kind." She took a bite out of it, and raspberry jelly squirted out and dripped down the side of her mouth. "Yum," she wiped her mouth with the napkin. "This is such a great surprise. Are you done with work today? Did you talk with Howard? Any news?" She asked as if Anthony was a client and she was dying to get as much out of him as possible.

Anthony proceeded to tell her about his day. "I told Nick that I won't be in to work until this big mess gets resolved. I then went to the hospital to see Howard. He is doing better. I told him I was going to stop by later and bring him some things. I then went to North Olmsted and was able to get an apartment."

Lisa, shocked, started to choke on the last bite of her doughnut. She took a sip of coffee and cleared her throat.

"You got an apartment? What's that mean, you are moving out?"

"I'm moving out tonight, to be exact. I can't stay with you anymore, Lisa. I don't want you to get hurt. It would be better this way." *Better for whom?* she thought.

"Okay," she groused. "I didn't think that you would move out already. I take it then that you received the check?"

"Yes, I did."

"When?"

"Yesterday. I forgot to mention it. So I was hoping that you can tell me how much I owe you, so that way I can return the money to you. I was also hoping that I could buy the Hummer from you. I really like that car."

She took out a piece of paper from the little sticky notes she had on her desk and wrote something down on it, and then handed it back to him. *I can't believe he used me!* She was mad as hell, and felt her body heat rise along with her blood pressure. Anthony looked at a big zero on the piece of paper and asked, "What do you mean zero?"

"You don't owe me anything. I don't want or need your money. You can have the Hummer. I don't need it. I will have the title transferred to your name as soon as I can so you can get the insurance for it in your name." she replied as politely as she could, not wanting to show her anger.

"I have to give you something!" he protested. "I appreciate it, but I have the money for it. And to tell you the truth, I really don't want the charity."

"I told you I wanted to help you out pro bono. It's a way for me to give back to the community. Don't worry about it."

"I need to go furniture shopping," he said, wanting to switch the subject. "I could use the company. Would you like to come with me? Then maybe we can get some dinner. I will take you out." He smiled that gorgeous smile of his and she couldn't help but smile back at him.

"Sure. Why not! What time do you want to go?"

"Can you take the rest of the day off?"

"Sure. Let me just put my things away, and we can go." She put the folders that were on her desk into her briefcase. They left her office and got into the Hummer.

"What do you need to get?"

"The kitchen has all appliances except a microwave and a coffee pot. I'll need a living room set and a bedroom set. Do you know if there is anywhere we can go that could deliver everything right away?"

"What is your hurry, exactly?" she asked as he drove onto I-71 South.

"I just don't want anything to happen to you." She rolled her eyes. *Yeah sure, it's more like you don't need me anymore. And to think I was ready to leave Rob in the past where he belonged and move on with my life with Anthony. I got played again! What is wrong with me?*

"What makes you think that anything will happen to me?"

"I just think that whoever is doing all of this won't stop until I move out of your place. He warned me twice and almost killed Howard." She thought about it for a minute.

"You think that this is all about me? I don't see how any of this could be related to me."

"I don't know. I don't get any of it. I am taking advice from your friend, Tucker."

Really? At least now I see the difference between Rob and Anthony. Rob would protect me by making sure he is with me, whereas Anthony would prefer to stay away. I think that Anthony no longer wants to be with me and is making "to protect me" an excuse to leave. Which is fine with me. I am better off by myself anyway.

"There is a furniture place by Great Northern Mall, we can go there first," she said, as he passed the airport exit and continued onto I-480 West. Without another word, he continued to drive until he parked the car in front of the furniture store.

"Come on," he said with a smile. "Time to do some shopping!" They walked throughout the store and looked around until a salesperson joined them.

"Do you need any help?" a man in a suit asked as he approached them.

"Would you guys be able to deliver right away?"

"If you choose something that we have here in stock, then yes, I can have someone deliver it tonight," the salesman replied.

"Great," Anthony continued, "I need a living room set and a bedroom set. So I will take whatever you have available that you could deliver."

"Sir, don't you want to look around first?" the man asked.

"Show me what you have in stock and I will pick something from it."

The man nodded and said, "Follow me." He led them to his desk and turned the computer towards Anthony. He pulled up living room sets first, and showed them the ones that were available.

"This one is perfect," Anthony said, as he pointed to a picture of two brown suede couches and a wooden coffee table. He turned to Lisa and asked, "What do you think?"

"It looks good," she replied, but could care less because all she could think about was Anthony using her.

The salesman marked the set and then showed him the bedroom suites next. Anthony picked one out in no time, and before they knew it, they were out the door. It was almost 5 and Anthony needed to get to the hospital to drop off the things for Howard. He dropped Lisa off at her office first so she could grab her car. They made plans to meet at her place at about 6. The new furniture would be arriving at about 8 that night so he would have about an hour to pack up his belongings from Lisa's. He dropped off the things for Howard and told him that he would visit with him in the morning.

It was dark out in the hospital parking lot, and he didn't notice the white envelope that was pressed to the windshield by the wiper blade until he turned on the Hummer. He eyed the envelope and opened the driver side window. He stuck his hand out and grabbed it. He heard his heart pounding in his chest as he quickly closed the window and made sure the doors were all locked. He opened the envelope and pulled out what he already knew would be another threat. This one stated: *LEAVE NOW BEFORE IT'S TOO LATE.* He immediately called Detective Frank and told him what he had found on his car. The detective said that he would meet up with him at Lisa's place in twenty minutes.

The detective was sitting with Lisa when Anthony came into the apartment. Without even taking his coat off, he handed the envelope to Frank.

"I'll take this back with me and give it to my forensics team. This person, though, is really good. We haven't come up with anything at Mr. Filiere's place, and the knife that was used was clean. I don't know what you did to this person, but I have had enough!" Detective Frank said as he pointed his finger at Anthony. "This is not a game, and if you are sending these threats to yourself, you'll be back in prison in no time!"

"I didn't do anything!" Anthony exclaimed. "I don't know who or why someone is making me suffer." Anthony shook his head.

"I have been talking with family members of the girls that were murdered a few years ago." Frank said. "There is one man who kind of struck a nerve with me, and I am keeping a close eye on him. You are staying here, correct?"

"Actually, I'm moving out tonight. I'm renting an apartment in North Olmsted."

"Okay, write me down the address, and I will have someone tail you, so don't get alarmed if you see someone following you," Detective Frank said, as Anthony handed him a piece of paper with his new address on it. "Make sure you call me if anything else happens. I am going to go now and pay Mr. Filiere a visit." Anthony and Lisa walked him to the door and locked it when he left.

"I can't believe this!" he angrily shouted as he followed Lisa to the kitchen where she poured herself another cup of coffee.

"Do you want anything to eat before we get going?" she asked him.

"No, thanks. I'm going to go and pack up all of my things," he replied and walked to his room. He threw all of his clothes in garbage bags and hauled everything out of the room and into the livingroom. Lisa helped him carry everything out into the Hummer.

"This is a good way to get in some exercise," Lisa said on their fourth and final trip to the Hummer."

"Yes it is," Anthony laughed out loud as he closed the back of the Hummer. "Thank you." He bent down and kissed her on the lips. "How about I make us dinner tomorrow night at the new place?"

Surprised, Lisa replied, "I would like that very much."

"Great. I'll call you later. You aren't going anywhere tonight are you?

"No. Jo is going to stop by a little later. Don't worry, I'll be fine." He gave her a hug and another quick kiss, and she watched him leave the garage.

Chapter 17

He stopped at Walmart to buy the coffee pot, microwave, pillows, bed sheets, a couple of blankets, and some bathroom towels, a few other necessities like dishes and cleaning supplies, and went to his new home. He was able to unload the Hummer before the furniture arrived.

It was 11 p.m. and everything was in its place. He made himself a pot of coffee and rested for a few minutes on his new couch. He knew he would never sleep well until he had figured everything out. The police department was as clueless as he was. He went through the boxes and took out the files on the three murdered women, and tried to come up with a common link. He got out a piece of paper and made a chart. He put the three women's names at the top and started writing the things that he remembered about each one. How and where they met, how long they dated, where they went out on dates, and everything else that he could possibly come up with. When he finished, he stared at the sheet of paper. The only thing that was common was that he met all three at the same bar that he used to hang out in. *It's a start!* he thought as he put everything away and then poured himself another cup of coffee.

Detective Frank had paid Howard a visit at the hospital, and unfortunately Howard still couldn't remember anything that had happened. The doctor told him that it might be a while before Howard could remember. He went through a great deal of stress and his mind, for the time being, has blocked it all out. Detective Frank stopped by the security office and asked to view the security camera videotape of that afternoon. Anthony told him where he was parked and he wanted to see if he would be able to see anyone on the tape dropping that note on the car. He spent the next couple of hours looking at the video from the parking lot. He saw the Hummer enter and exit, but that was all the video showed from this camera. He looked at the other one that was on the other side of the building and that camera didn't show anything, either. The hospital didn't have cameras set up in the garage, so he was unable to see anyone walking by the car. He ran the video over and over again, and something struck him as odd. A black Chevy Malibu had gone in through the front entrance and just a few minutes later, the same car had exited on the other side of the garage. It was strange to him that the car basically just entered and almost right away left. He was able to see the license plate of the car and he wrote it down in his notebook. He had thanked the security officer and left. He wanted to run this plate at the station, and he still needed to get the note to forensics.

The next morning, Anthony woke up to his phone ringing. He picked up the phone; 10 a.m. *Crap!* He got up off the couch that he had fallen asleep on. He walked into the kitchen and turned on the coffee pot. He checked his phone and saw that he had missed four phone calls. One from Howard, one from Detective Frank, and two from Lisa who had left a message to give her a call back. He called Howard first.

"How are you?" he asked Howard.

"I'm okay, bored. Did I miss anything?"

"I will come and visit with you today. Then I'll give you the lowdown," Anthony replied. "Do you want me to bring you anything?"

"I don't know, they have me on some kind of liquid diet so I can't eat anything. Maybe you can bring me something more to read. I have read through all of those magazines that you brought me yesterday. I have to go, the doctor just came in." Howard hung up.

Anthony called Lisa next.

"Hi, how are you?" Anthony asked.

"Hi. I called you this morning and you didn't pick up." Lisa said.

"I was passed out, sorry I didn't hear the phone ring."

"Rough night?"

"Yeah. I was up late going through all of those files. I wanted to see if there was anything that I missed."

"And?"

"Nothing," he replied. "Are we on for dinner?"

"Sure. What time would you like me to come over?" Lisa asked.

"How about 7?"

"7 it is. I will see you later then, bye." She hung up the phone and his rang again,

"Hello," he answered.

"It's Detective Frank. There were no fingerprints, other than yours, or any DNA on the card that you gave me yesterday. Just wanted to let you know. We are going to have to work together on this. What are your plans today?"

"I'm not going in to work. I will go to the hospital and I plan on stopping by at a bar to catch up with some old friends. I will be home by 7 tonight. I have plans with Lisa," Anthony replied.

"Okay. Don't forget that I have someone following you." Detective Frank hung up.

Anthony poured himself a cup of coffee. *Darn it! I forgot to buy a toaster. I'll have to go to the grocery store anyways. Hopefully I'll remember to get one.* He didn't buy anything to eat yesterday, except for bread. *At least I remembered to get the coffee pot and a couple of cups.* He drank his cup of coffee, and decided to head over to Target. It took him a couple of hours to get everything that he thought that he needed. He even bought a rug set for the bathroom. From there, he went to Giant Eagle to buy some groceries and some wine. He wanted everything to go well tonight with Lisa. He was hoping that she would spend the night. He dropped everything off at home, except for the newspaper and a couple of books that he was taking to Howard.

It was almost 5 when he left the hospital. He didn't notice anyone following him and he wondered if Detective Frank had lied about that. He was a little pressed for time since he was making dinner but he decided to stop by the bar anyway. He hoped that the owners haven't changed and that the same bartender was still there. He parked on the street and stepped out of the car. He looked around and didn't see anyone. It was dark out. He opened the door to the bar and walked in. To his excitement, the place looked exactly the same. The two booths that were on the right side were empty, but the few tables were occupied. There was one empty wooden stool at the bar and he quickly walked over to claim it.

"The place seems busy," Anthony said, as a bartender he didn't recognize came over to him.

"It's Happy Hour here. Every beer is two bucks, so we get pretty busy," the bartender replied, and then asked "what can I get you?"

"I'll take a Stella, please," Anthony answered and the bartender obliged. The place was too busy for him to talk with the only bartender and Anthony was disappointed. He drank his beer, left a $5 bill on the bar and exited. As he opened the door, he bumped into someone. Another man, seemed to be his age, without a word, stepped back a little to let Anthony out.

"Thanks," Anthony said, as he moved out onto the sidewalk. The man nodded and Anthony went to the Hummer. The man just stood by the door and watched and he gave Anthony the creeps. He got into the Hummer and locked the doors. He put on his seatbelt, turned on the car but watched the man who was still standing by the door. He didn't look familiar to him, yet oddly enough, he felt as if he knew him. The man lit up a cigarette. He was wearing jeans and a black coat. He had worn a cap that obscured his face. He did notice that he was pretty tan. *Maybe it's that detective that's supposed to follow me,* he thought, as he started to drive.

Once home, Anthony started to cook dinner. He was making pasta carbonara. It was 6 p.m. and he had plenty of time to finish it before Lisa would arrive. While everything was cooking away on the stove, he tore up the lettuce and put it in the refrigerator. He had bought some kind of frozen bread loaf that he put in the oven to heat up. Once everything was done and ready in the kitchen, he went to get ready.

Lisa was rummaging through her closet and was aggravated that she couldn't find anything that she felt like wearing. They were having dinner at his apartment so she wanted to look casual but sexy. *Look at the mess I made,* she thought as she grabbed a red sweater peering through a pile of clothes she had dropped on the floor from her closet. She saw a pair of dark denim jeans in another pile. *I guess this will have to do.* By the time she finished getting ready, it was time for her to leave. As much as she hated to leave her tornado hit room as it was, she didn't want to be late.

Anthony let her in and told her to get comfortable. She took her shoes and coat off and sat down on one of the couches, while he went to the kitchen to get everything.

"Do you need any help with anything?" she called out to him.

"No thanks. You just stay there and I'll bring everything out," he responded as he put the pasta on a couple of plates. He dressed the salad, and took the bread out of the oven. With a couple of trips, he had everything on the coffee table in front of Lisa. "Voila!" He opened the bottle of red wine and poured each of them a glass. He sat down on the opposite couch and dug in.

"Wow, this is great. You made this all yourself?"

"Yes, I did," he said proudly with a smile. "I couldn't remember the recipe but I Googled it. It's fast and easy. How was your day?"

"It was okay. I went through a couple of files for two clients I have, and I met with two more today."

"That's good. At least you're busy."

"What did you do today?"

"I visited with Howard for a while, and did some more shopping. Would you like some more?" He asked her as she put the last bite of the pasta in her mouth. She shook her head and swallowed.

"No, thanks, that was plenty."

"Did you notice anyone outside? I came across someone today. I thought maybe it's the detective that's supposed to be following me."

"I didn't see anyone, or notice anything out of place," she replied. "This is a cute little place. The furniture fits in perfectly." She leaned back on the couch and relaxed. She smiled and watched Anthony clear the table. "Do you want any help?"

"Nope, you just sit and relax. It'll only take a minute," he replied as he put the dishes in the kitchen sink.

"I can get used to this," she said as he sat next to her on the couch.

"Get used to what exactly?"

"You cooking for me and cleaning it all up," she laughed.

"You are one amazing woman. You deserve to be lavished upon." He leaned in and kissed her.

That night, he showed her not only that he liked her, but that he loved her. He had never made such passionate love with anyone. Their strong feelings for each other and the sensations they both felt that night were beyond incredible. They finally fell asleep in each other's arms and before they knew it, her cell phone alarm went off. She grabbed it off the nightstand and pressed the off button. She looked over and Anthony was awake and smiling at her.

"I can get used to this," he said as he started to kiss her neck. As much as she wanted to stay, she had an appointment with a new client at eight.

"Me, too." She moaned. "But I really need to go. I have to be in at 8 and I need to go home and get ready."

"Okay." He disappointedly moved off to the side. "You want to have dinner again tonight?"

"Sure, I'll call you when I am done with work," she replied as she slid off the bed and put her clothes on. "I'm just going to use the bathroom real quick, and then I'm going to leave."

Anthony didn't want to get up, so he stayed in bed. In a few minutes, Lisa peered through the doorway, said goodbye and left. Anthony fell back asleep.

He spent all night in his Chevy, watching Anthony's apartment. *I can't believe she stayed there all night long.* He yawned as he watched her get into her car. He was angry and didn't think that he could wait any longer to cross her path. *Man, would she be shocked to see me. I can't wait 'til I see the look on her face! I can't believe that she not only helped him get out of prison, but is now screwing him as well. And what's with Tucker? He has been in touch with Lisa. I wonder if she screwed him, too. Well, I am going to screw all of them at the end! One by one, they will all die, and soon, really, really, soon.* He turned on his car and pulled out of the parking lot. He needed to go home and get some sleep. He needed to be rested and alert. *Tonight is going to be one hell of a night!*

Chapter 18

It was 10 a.m. and Rob Tucker was sitting in his car parked across the street from the house that he was watching. *Come on, get up already,* he thought to himself as he waited for the man to leave. He took the last couple of days off just so he could find him, and now that he has him, he isn't planning on losing him. He thought about going into the house and killing him, but he wasn't going to risk it, at least not yet. He had to figure out a way to get him without implicating himself. *No one needs to know what I had done.* He then thought about telling Lisa the truth, but he just couldn't, not when his secret was so much bigger than hers. For now, the plan was just to watch his every move. The only thing he knew, was that he wasn't going to let anyone else get hurt. His guilty conscience just couldn't take it anymore. He should of never helped Jerry out. He knew that Jerry murdered the women and he helped him out by making sure that Anthony was convicted. Not only did Rob do that, but he helped him "commit" suicide and helped him get to Mexico where he still should be. *I should have known that he'd be back, since Anthony was released, but how did he even find out? I haven't heard from him since he disappeared.*

The Chevy Malibu Detective Frank looked up was reported stolen by the owner two weeks ago. He put out an APB on the vehicle, but the car still was not found. He was going absolutely nowhere with this case, and his frustration was visible to everyone at the station. He just couldn't tie anything together. He sat at his desk and read his notes over and over. He looked at a blurry picture of the man who was driving the car, and he wondered, if at all, any of this was connected. His phone rang, and he answered, "Detective Frank."

"Detective, this is Howard Filiere. I remembered some things, and thought I should give you a call."

"That's great news! Mr. Filiere, I'll come there right away. I should be there within 15 minutes." Frank hung up the phone and dashed out of the office. He couldn't wait to hear what Howard remembered, and he hoped that he was able to see the culprit who attacked him.

Howard was lying in his bed trying to make sense of the things that he was starting to remember. The doctor had told him that the images, at first, would be somewhat confusing. He was tired from thinking and fell asleep before the detective arrived.

Anthony had finally gotten up out of bed and had made himself a cup of coffee. He put a couple of pieces of bread in the toaster and looked out in the backyard through the little window above the sink. *What a great view*, he sarcastically thought, as he was able to directly see into the livingroom of the apartment next to his. He drank his coffee and ate the toast as he planned out his day. He was going to take his mom some lunch and then he was going to visit Howard. After that, he planned on going back to the bar. He packed his mom some of the pasta he had made the night before, and left the apartment.

As he drove to the nursing home, he noticed a small, red vehicle following him. This made him nervous and yet relieved at the same time. He parked the Hummer in the parking lot, grabbed the bag of food on the passenger seat and stepped out. The red car parked a few spaces back. Anthony wondered if he should go over there and introduce himself. He stared at the car and waited a minute to see if the man would get out. He rolled his eyes as no movement had been made by the man, and he entered the home. He walked over to his mother's room, knocked, and entered an empty room. He checked the bathroom and with his mom out of sight, he went to the receptionist.

"Where is my mother?" Anthony asked the short, red-haired, pudgy lady at the desk.

"Your name, sir?" she asked back with the same attitude that she had received from Anthony.

"Anthony Rozman, my mother's name is Mary," he answered, as the lady put something into the computer, waited a second, and then told Anthony that she would be right back. She went down the hall and a few minutes later returned with an elderly man at her side.

"Mr. Rozman, my name is Dr. Felix, and I am the chief of staff of the nursing home." He shook his hand. "I need to talk to you, so could you please follow me to my office." Anthony nodded and followed him. He knew what he was going to tell him.

The doctor closed the office door and told Anthony to have a seat.

"There is no easy way for me to say this."

"You don't need to say it. I know. My mother is dead, isn't she?" Anthony asked.

"Yes, I'm sorry. She had a stroke early this morning, I was just getting ready to give Miss Furrow a call. She was listed as having power of attorney. Your mom's body has been taken to the funeral home, and her belongings are still here. Someone will bring them out to you before you leave." Dr. Felix made a call and within minutes the receptionist brought over her mom's things.

"I really am sorry about your mom," she said as she handed him a couple of bags. "These are all of her belongings."

"Thank you," Anthony said. He shook their hands and left the home heartbroken. As he walked to the car he began to cry. He knew this day would one day come, but he wanted his mom around just a little longer. He missed so much of the last five years, and there was nothing that he could do to turn back the clock.

He put his mom's things in the back of the Hummer. Through his tears, he saw the man who was driving the red car sitting on the hood, smoking a cigarette. *Is it the same man I ran into at the bar?* Anthony entered the vehicle. He waited a couple of minutes to see if the man would come over to him, but he didn't. When he looked in the rearview mirror, he saw the man getting into the car. Anthony left the parking lot and drove around for miles. He didn't answer his phone when it rang and just drove. He had no idea what time it was or where he was going. It was as if someone else was driving and he just went with it. When the car finally came to a halt, he wiped the tears from his eyes and looked straight ahead at a place where his mom used to take him when he was a little boy. He was parked right in front of the Cleveland Mounted Police Station. He smiled as his mind went back in time.

"Come on, let's go see the horses," his mom would say after breakfast on a Saturday morning. His mom would take him to the

Mounted Police Station where they wound spend a couple of hours feeding and petting the horses. Every so often, an officer would even give him a ride. His mom always looked so happy when she was here. That's how they used to spend time with each other, just the two of them. He now knew that his mom was fine and happy.

A bald, bulky, police officer walked over to the Hummer and knocked on the window. Anthony rolled open the window and the officer asked, "Everything okay?"

"Yes, everything is fine, sir. I just stopped here for a minute," Anthony replied and smiled. "Have a good day, officer," he said as he pulled out on the street, as the officer watched him depart.

He looked at the clock that read 3:28. "Shit!" he said to himself. "I need to go see Howard." Twenty minutes later, he was at the hospital, knocking on the door to Howard's room.

"Anthony! Where have you been? I called you a bunch of times! I remembered what happened. I saw the guy. Detective Frank left a little bit ago with the sketch artist. I hope they can get him now."

"That's great news! I hope they do, too." Anthony said sullenly. "What did the guy look like?"

"He was about your age, and a little shorter than you. He had brown hair, and brown eyes. To tell you the truth, Anthony, he kind of looked like you. Except that he was darker in skin tone. When I was describing the guy to the sketch artist and when she showed me and the detective the picture she drew, we were both stunned. We thought she drew a picture of you. The only thing that was different was that he had longer, wavy hair and he was darker. I spent 20 minutes convincing the detective that it wasn't you."

"That's interesting," Anthony replied. "Maybe your mind is all mixed up."

"It's a possibility. But the images are so real, and I am reliving the events over and over."He looked over at Anthony whose mind seemed so far away. "What's wrong with you?"

"I went to the nursing home to visit my mom earlier, and was informed that she died earlier this morning," Anthony replied. "I feel like crap. I didn't expect her to die yet, you know?"

"I'm so sorry, Anthony. This is just horrible news. How did she die?"

"The doctor told me that she had a stroke, but I don't know. He said that the body was taken to a funeral home. I didn't even ask which one. I should call Lisa." He looked in his coat pockets and couldn't find his phone. "I think I left the phone in the car." Anthony shook his head in anguish. "Sorry Howard, I need to go. I'll call you later," Anthony rushed out of the room.

This day can't possibly get any worse than it is, he thought as he got back into the Hummer. He turned it on and looked for the phone. *Come on, where is it?* He checked the floor, under his seat, he looked in the glove compartment and no phone. He reached over and felt the floor under the passenger seat. *Yes! Got it.* He snatched it and looked at it. He missed a bunch of phone calls. He called Lisa back first but got no reply. He listened to a voicemail that she had left, and it was just a message that said call me back right away. He then called Detective Frank, and was told the same information that Howard had given him, except that he told him that his mother's body was retrieved from the funeral home and sent to the coroner's office. His mother's body would be autopsied. They want to make sure that there wasn't any foul play in her death. He turned the sound up on the phone, and headed home.

At home, he made himself some coffee and waited for Lisa to call him. He even sent her a few texts to which she had yet to reply.

Chapter 19

It was 5:00 p.m., and Rob Tucker was back at the same spot

he was that morning. Rob had spent all day following him, who was

in turn, tailing Anthony. He should have confronted him when he

saw him steal a little red car this morning, but he didn't. Rob wanted

to continue his surveillance and see what his next move was. *I guess*

he got bored with Anthony and went home. Or, maybe not, he

thought as the man walked back out of the house and into the car.

His tires squealed as he pulled out of the driveway, Rob turned on

his car and carefully followed. The man got off the freeway and

headed down Superior Avenue. *Where are we going now?* Rob

thought as he drove a couple of cars behind him. He drove into the

garage at East Ninth and Rob knew exactly who the man was going

to spy on next. Rob parked on the street and waited a few minutes

before driving the car into the garage and parking his vehicle. He

was able to see the red car from where he was, so he waited and

watched. Rob wondered if he would actually make a move and go

see Lisa. *You go up, and so do I. Lisa isn't going to get hurt tonight, not on my watch,* he thought as he watched him not moving from the car.

Lisa came home from work and poured herself a glass of wine. She didn't know how she was going to break it to Anthony that his mother had passed. The director of the nursing home had called her today to inform her. She didn't want to hurt him. She couldn't even pick up the phone when he called her. *I am such a wuss,* she thought as she gulped down the wine and heard a knock on the door. *Here he comes.* She walked over to the door and opened it. He quickly pushed pass her and locked the door behind himself.

"Oh my God!" she exclaimed. "Jerry?" she fainted and hit the floor. Jerry had so many different visions of how she was going to react when she realized that he was still alive, but her fainting wasn't one of them. He picked her up and carried her to the couch, where he laid her down. He went to the kitchen and grabbed a Stella out of her fridge. He popped the bottle open and chugged. He sat down on the other couch and watched her lie there.

Meanwhile, Anthony was still at home and waiting to hear from Lisa. He wondered why she hadn't replied. He decided to call Jo.

"Hi, Jo," he said when she answered. "It's Anthony. How are you?"

"I'm okay," she replied, "I heard about your mom. Please accept my condolences."

"Thank you. How do you know about my mom?" he asked surprised. He didn't even tell Lisa about it.

"I talked to Lisa, not too long ago," Jo replied, hoping that she doesn't cause any trouble for Lisa. Lisa didn't tell her not to say anything.

"Oh. Do you know where she's at? I've been trying to get ahold of her and she isn't replying."

"She's probably home now. I talked to her as she was leaving her office."

"Thanks," Anthony said. "I'll talk to you soon. Have a good night."

"Night. Let me know if you need anything," she said as he disconnected the phone call.

He didn't know if he should just drive over to Lisa's or wait for her call. He was feeling very nervous and he wasn't sure if it was because his mom died, or because Lisa hadn't replied yet. He decided to take a shower and drive over there.

Lisa was slowly coming to, and when she opened her eyes, she saw Jerry sitting on the

other couch. She rubbed her eyes and looked there again hoping that she was imagining him being there.

"I'm alive, Lisa," he said casually, "did you miss me? I missed you."

"But how?" She asked confused as she sat up. "The car exploded with you in it?"

"The car exploded, but I didn't, those weren't my ashes. I see you have been busy. You lied to me, Lisa." His tone was angry.

"I didn't lie," she replied.

"I can't believe you helped him get out. I am totally disappointed in you." He shook his head. "Did you tell him that I did it? Did you tell him everything?"

"No, I didn't. I didn't tell him anything about you," she answered still in disbelief that Jerry was sitting right across from her. "Why did you come back? You're the one that's been sending those threats? Oh my God, you stabbed Howard?! Did you kill his mom, too? Why? Why are you doing this? "

"If he stayed in jail, I wouldn't have done shit. But no, you had to go out of your way to help him! Not only that, you let him stay here! This is going to end tonight."

"What are you going to do, kill me? Kill Anthony? How are you planning to do that?" she nervously asked him as she dug around for her phone so that she can call 911.

"You looking for this?" He showed her the phone. "You aren't calling anyone." He took his gun out of his pocket and put it on his lap. "Don't make me use it Lisa, you know very well I would."

Rob Tucker watched Anthony get out of his car and take the elevator. He didn't see Jerry make a move out of the car, so he continued to wait and watch the red car.

. "I wonder what you're up to?" Rob said to himself. "I can be here all night long."

Anthony knocked on the door and waited for Lisa to open it.

"Get the door and let him in," Jerry said, and got up. With his gun in hand, he positioned himself behind the door where only Lisa could see him.

She opened the door, and before she could even say anything, Anthony barged in yelling.

"I have been calling you all day long! Why haven't you called me back?"

The door slammed shut behind him and Anthony turned around.

"Who are you?" he asked the man he had run into before. "What are you doing here?"

"I'm your worst nightmare," Jerry said, as he pointed the gun at him. "Sit down and be quiet. You aren't the only one that's in a bad mood." He grabbed a bag that was by the door and flung it to Lisa. "Lisa, take the rope out and tie his wrists and ankles."

Lisa did as ordered. She tied the wrists first, and Jerry checked it as she tied the ankles.

"I'm sorry," she whispered in Anthony's ear before she stepped back.

Jerry pushed Anthony back and he landed on the couch.

"Lisa, sit right next to him so I can tie you up as well." Jerry tied her hands first and then her ankles. Once he was done, he said, "there, all set." He stood in front of them and crossed his arms.

"Who are you, and what the hell do you want?" Anthony probed.

Jerry smiled at the question and looked at Lisa,

"You want to tell him, or shall I? Actually, I want to hear you tell him." He took a seat on the couch opposite them. "Come on, start at the beginning, I want Anthony to know it all before I kill him." Lisa shivered as Jerry flashed an evil smile.

"What exactly do you want me to tell him?" Lisa asked.

"Everything. I want you to tell him the whole truth. So start." She turned herself at an angle so that she could watch Anthony's reaction. She was about to tell him everything that she knew.

"This is your half-brother, Jerry."

"I thought you said that he was dead."

"I was wrong, apparently. I thought that he was, too. I thought that he committed suicide as he blew up his car."

"Who else am I?" Jerry intervened.

"Jerry used to be someone I dated."

"Thank you," Jerry said. Anthony was confused and interrupted,

"You two used to be together, and you are my half-brother. I still don't understand what that has to do with me being tied up!"

"Jerry killed those three women and framed you for it," Lisa quickly blurted out.

"Why?" Anthony was even more confused. "I didn't do anything to you. I didn't even know that I had a brother?"

"Yeah, I was well aware of that. My father, the bastard. Did you know that you and I were born on the same day? At the same hospital? Just by two different women." Anthony and Lisa quietly watched Jerry talk. "He was such a jerk. He was a drunken loser that spent every day abusing me. Mentally, physically. He would come home from a bar and start yelling at me. 'You,' he'd say, 'you ruined my life! It's all your fault!' He blamed me, not himself, for getting my mother pregnant. He even admitted to me that he was forced into marrying my mother. He always wished that I was you. After my mom died, he became even worse. All he did was talk about you and your mother. My sister ran away from home when she was fifteen years old just to get away from the creep!"

"I'm sorry," Anthony said. "It must have been hard for you. But that's still not my fault, and Lisa has nothing to do with this, so don't hurt her!"

"Like how I have ruined my father's life, you have ruined mine. I wanted you to suffer, like I did. And Lisa, Lisa, Lisa. She knew that I did it. She knew all of it and she failed me. She promised me that she would never tell anyone, and what does she do? She gets you out of prison,"

"I thought that you were dead!" Lisa screamed.

"You knew he did it?! And you didn't tell me! How could you not tell me?" Anthony cried out.

"I'm sorry. I was going to tell you." Lisa lowered her voice, embarrassed. "Please, forgive me."

"When? When were you going to tell me all of this?" Anthony was frustrated and disappointed in Lisa. He knew all along that she was hiding something from him and he finally found out what that was. He knew that deep down there was a reason to why she has been so kind toward him. *She probably doesn't do any pro-bono work. What a fucking moron I am to believe that she actually cared for me!*

"I knew that you would tell him, Lisa. That's why I came back. Now I am going to kill the both of you and disappear again!" Jerry yelled out. He was sick of watching them talk back and forth. *I'm here, too. This isn't about the two of you. It's about me!*

Chapter 20

Back in the garage, Rob was sick of waiting around, and was going to confront him once and for all. He stepped out of his car and carefully walked over to the parked car. As he got closer to the car, he saw that something wasn't right. He dashed to the car and looked through the window. "Son of a bitch! He isn't even here. Shit!" He took his burner phone out and called 9-1-1.

"9-1-1, what's your emergency?"

"I just saw a man with a gun on the elevator at the Nine. You need to get someone out here as fast as possible."

"Do you know what floor he got off?"

"Nineteenth," Rob said and hung up. He went into the elevator and pressed 19. He hoped that he wasn't late.

He kicked in the door to her loft and barged in. They all turned and saw Rob, with gun in hand aiming it at Jerry.

"It's all over. Put the gun down, Jerry. The police are on their way," he demanded and Jerry laughed.

"Ha, ha, ha, that's funny coming from you, cousin, Rob," Lisa gasped. "Yes, you heard right, Lisa. Rob is my cousin." He turned his head and faced Rob again. "I was just about to shoot the both of them and place the gun in Anthony's hand. You know, murder-suicide."

"I'm serious," Rob said. "I'm not going to help you this time. I should have never helped you in the first place."

"What?" Lisa cried out. "You helped him? You didn't tell me? Even after I told you?"

Well now, now you should know exactly how betrayed I feel, Anthony thought, as he quietly sat there. He felt as if he was having a nightmare, and he prayed that he would soon wake up.

"Now that's disappointing, Lisa. I guess we all had a secret we wanted to bury. And now it will all end," Jerry said as he pulled the trigger and Rob hit the floor.

"Nooo!" Lisa screamed as the tears began to flow down her cheeks.

"You're next!" Jerry pointed the gun at Anthony and just as he pulled the trigger, she saw Jerry fall down. A swarm of policemen stormed in. Lisa looked at Anthony who was slumped on the sofa and bleeding from the shoulder. Stunned, she watched as EMS put Rob on a stretcher and then Anthony.

"You all right?" a policeman asked her.

"Uh, yeah, I'm not hurt," she answered as the policeman untied her. "Thank you," she mumbled and stood up. She walked over to where Jerry was lying. "Is he dead?" she asked Detective Frank, who was observing the body and jotting down notes.

"Yes, he is. We came at the right moment. The officer shot him just when he pulled the trigger. Anthony got lucky that the bullet didn't hit him in the head. Why don't you go have a seat and I'll be with you shortly," he instructed her and she complied. Anthony and Rob were both gone, and on the way to the hospital. Lisa watched as they put Jerry in a body bag and zipped it. Detective Frank sat by her and started the questioning,

"Why don't you tell me what happened."

"I came home from work. I poured myself a glass of wine and I heard a knock on the door. I assumed that it was Anthony. When I opened the door, Jerry pushed me in and locked the door behind him."

"You know him?"

"Yes, I do," she answered and continued, "I was shocked to see him. I thought that he was dead. Anthony came a short time after. He had us tied up and then proceeded to tell Anthony who he was, and why he was doing everything. He admitted to murdering the three women from before. He is the one who hurt Howard, too."

"Did he say why?"

"It turns out, that he and Anthony are half-brothers. He had a bad childhood and hated his father, so he took that hatred out on Anthony."

"And you knew him from before?" Detective Frank asked her recalling that she said she knew him.

"Yes, I did. He was, once, a good friend of mine."

"Did you know all along that he killed those women? That's a criminal offense."

"No. I didn't know, until tonight," she quickly responded, knowing full well that she could get in trouble. *I hope that Rob doesn't say anything.*

"How does Tucker fit into all of this?"

"That I don't know. Rob came in just before Jerry shot Anthony. What a mess."

"Well it's all over now," Detective Frank said. "I need to go to the hospital and question the both of them. Then I can finish the report and close the case. Just so you know, Mrs. Rozman had a stroke and died, so there wasn't any foul play." He put his notebook in his pocket and stood up. "If I have any other questions, I'll give you a call."

"Thanks, Detective Frank. I'm going to go to the hospital as well, so I will probably see you there." She watched the detective leave and looked around.

Many policemen were still there. Some were taking prints, some were taking pictures, and others were standing around and talking. She hoped that they wouldn't take too long, she really wanted to go to the hospital.

"Are we almost done yet?" she yelled out so everyone could hear her. An officer turned around and answered, "Not yet. Maybe another half hour."

"Thank you," Lisa said. She walked into the kitchen and made a pot of coffee. *I hope Rob and Anthony are doing okay.*

Detective Frank, at the hospital, questioned Anthony, whose story coincides with Lisa's. *What a nightmare for him. At least now he knows the who and the why,* he thought as he left Anthony's room and went down the hall to pay a visit to Rob. He knocked on the door and entered.

"How you holding up?" he asked Rob as he took a seat next to the bed.

"I'll be fine. The bullet went straight through my side. Did you kill him?"

"Yeah, he's dead." Detective Frank replied. "Glad it's all over with. This case was driving me nuts. All I need is your statement and I will get out of here."

"I decided to pay a visit to Lisa," Rob began to say, "I wanted to see how she was doing. We were very close, once, and since Anthony has been out of prison, I have been worried about her. When I went to the apartment I heard someone yelling so I barged right in. He shot me and all I remember is getting put on a stretcher." *Please, don't ask me anything else. I can't tell him that I knew Jerry and that he killed those women. If Frank finds out, I am screwed!*

"And with all of your training, you didn't call it in?" astounded, detective Frank asked.

"No, I didn't. I just wanted to get in there. It's a good thing that you guys showed up when you did. How did you know we were all there?"

"Someone called 911. We got there in the nick of time. He took a shot at Anthony. He'll be fine, too. He got hit in the shoulder. You guys got very lucky tonight. I'm going to go to the office now to write up the report. I'll see you soon." He stood up and as he walked out of the room, Lisa entered.

"They're done there already?" Detective Frank asked her.

"Yes," Lisa replied, "have a good night, Detective, and thanks again." He nodded and left.

"How are you?" she asked Rob as she walked over to him.

"I'll be fine. How are you?"

"A little confused, shocked, and relieved. Did they tell you Jerry's dead?"

"Yeah, I heard. That son of a bitch deserved what he got."

"How come you didn't tell me that you and Jerry were related? How come you didn't tell me that he was still alive and that you helped him fake his death? I told you that I knew him and that he committed the crimes."

"I couldn't do it, Lisa. I couldn't take the risk of having me go to prison. I didn't even know that you knew him until you told me your secret. I just couldn't tell you that we were related and that he was alive. I knew everything, and I, like you, didn't tell anyone. We have both been living with this horrible guilt for the last five years. I'm glad it all finally ended. We both had secrets we were hiding and I just couldn't be with you. I knew, because I loved you, that I would eventually tell you. And once I did, I knew that our relationship would change. I'm sorry, I really am."

"How did you know he was at my place, Rob?"

"I figured out it was him that day when you and I had our talk. When I found him I followed him around."

"You could have warned me," she retorted.

He pulled himself up a little. "I know, thought about it, and I didn't. I'm so sorry, I hope that you can one day forgive me. I really do care for you, Lisa."

"I know you do, Rob. You take care of yourself," she said. She leaned down and kissed him on his cheek.

Anthony was asleep and didn't hear Lisa come in. She pulled up a chair next to his bed and held his hand. She hoped that he could forgive her deceptions and she hoped that they would continue their relationship. She figured out tonight exactly who she loved. When Jerry shot Anthony all she could do was close her eyes and pray. She knew that he was the one that she couldn't live without.

"Hi," Anthony said when he opened his eyes and saw her sitting there.

"How are you?" she asked him.

"I'm a survivor," he replied. "How are you?"

"I think I'll be just fine. I'm sorry I didn't tell you about Jerry. I honestly didn't know he was alive. All these years, and I thought he was dead. He was my best friend. Before he supposedly committed suicide, he confessed the murders to me, and made me promise not to ever tell anyone."

"You should have told me, Lisa."

"I know, I'm so sorry," she said with regret. "Can you forgive me, Anthony?"

"Well, I'm not going to let the love of my life walk right out of it!" he said. Her face lit up and she smiled.

"Really? You mean it? You aren't just going to kick me to the curb?" she asked surprised to have heard what he just said.

"Oh, yeah. I can't wait to get out of here, and go home with you. I love you Lisa Furrow. But you have to promise me that, from now on, we only tell each other the truth, and there are no more secrets between us."

With happy tears forming in her eyes, she stood up from the chair that she was sitting on, she leaned over him and whispered, "I love you, too."

About the author

Anna Vucica, born in Cleveland, Ohio, is 38 years old. When she was two years old, her family moved to Croatia, the country where her family is originally from. She started school there, and when she was 10 years old, her family moved back to Cleveland. She has been living in Cleveland ever since, but visits her family in Croatia whenever she is able. Anna is married and has two beautiful girls that she hopes, like her, follow their dreams. She graduated from Cleveland State University with a psychology degree. Anna writes while working at her family's restaurant, and has written her second mystery novel in her adopted language. Using her psychology degree, and her remarkable creativity, she weaves a tale of cunning mystery that will captivate you until the very end.

Made in the USA
Middletown, DE
05 June 2021